Future School

Walk Like Lions

Eric Patterson

Cover Illustrated by Chris Wright

Avid Readers Publishing Group
Lakewood, California

Future School   Walk Like Lions

Avid Readers Publishing Group

http://www.avidreaderspg.com

ISBN-13: 978-1-61286-324-5

Printed in the United States

Acknowledgment

May all the glory go to Jesus for without Him, these words would have never been put to paper.

Chapter 1

Bridgette and her best friend, Sara, were skipping rope in the park when Bridgette's younger brother scampered over to greet them. By the expression on his face, Bridgette knew the long awaited letter had finally arrived, the letter that would ultimately decide her family's destiny, but most importantly, her own.

"It's here! It's here!" Tommy exclaimed. He stood only an arm's length away, yet he still screamed at the top of his lungs. Tommy was just as excited to learn about his future as the rest of the family. He hunched over, resting his hands on his exposed knee caps and panted like a thirsty German shepherd as he attempted to catch his breath.

Bridgette's heart almost leaped out of her chest. She and Sara stared at each other through golden rays of sunlight for a few long seconds. Finally, Bridgette swallowed and took a deep breath. "Well, I guess it's time," she said nervously.

Sara dropped her head. Her long brown hair hung over her face and covered her eyes. "Good luck," she said as she lifted her head and pulled her hair back with one hand.

"I'll let you know one way or the other," said Bridgette glumly.

"I'll be at home," said Sara. "Just give me a call as soon as you find out." She had little hope left in her voice.

Tommy raced ahead, eager to prove his swiftness. The sudden burst of speed sparked the competitiveness in Bridgette. She chased after her pesky little brother through the well-groomed grass, gaining ground with every determined stride.

When they arrived at their home gasping for air, Bridgette had clearly defeated Tommy once again. They quickly scrambled into their cozy little apartment building, which stood in a lower class neighborhood near Tacoma, Washington.

The apartment building was a small complex, containing only six separate dwellings. Tenants were always moving, mostly

1

due to evictions, so Bridgette's family could never really get to know their neighbors very well.

Bridgette dashed into the living room where her parents waited anxiously huddled on the brown sofa that had an orange spot on it. As if Bridgette were their queen, her loving parents stood and bowed their heads. Following their eyes, Bridgette stared down at the coffee table where the lone letter lay. She gazed upon the white envelope that sealed her fate. She studied it and then read the print on the upper left corner. It stated: THE LAS VEGAS SCHOOL OF EXCELLENCE, EDUCATING THE BRIGHT MINDS OF TOMORROW.

"Go ahead and open it, Sweetheart," urged her father.

"Yeah, hurry up already!" blurted Tommy, who had pounced down on the couch, half covering the orange spot he had caused while experimenting with bleach one day.

Bridgette hesitated. She dreaded what the future might hold in store for her. She feared the answer that lay hidden behind the thin walls of the envelope. Finally, she leaned over and scooped it up with trembling fingers. She peeled a corner section away and slid her finger inside. Pulling her pinky across, she ripped the rest of the sealed envelope apart. Carefully, she removed the letter and held it tightly to her chest, the whole time squeezing her eyes shut. She prayed one final time as she blindly unfolded the letter. Opening one eye, she spotted the first word written in big bold letters: CONGRATULATIONS! Her heart sank. She couldn't read any further. She dropped the letter, watched it cartwheel off the edge of the table, and then burst out of the room with tears trickling down her flushed cheeks. The slam of her bedroom door echoed throughout the thin walls of the building followed by the squeak of her bedsprings and her rhythmic blubbering.

Not seeming to notice their daughter's anguish, Bridgette's parents embraced each other as if their prayers had finally been answered. Their twelve-year-old daughter had just been accepted to the most exclusive school in the world.

The Las Vegas School of Excellence recruited only the brightest young minds. It had the reputation of graduating America's finest geniuses. Rumor had it that something incredible had been discovered, and all new students would be educated beyond their wildest imaginations.

Bridgette's parents were proud of their daughter and excited that she would be attending the school, but they were also thrilled about relocating to Las Vegas, Nevada - not only that, but the Las Vegas School of Excellence was paying for everything, including a new home.

Their new house would have three bedrooms, unlike the apartment they lived in now, which only contained two. Tommy and Bridgette would no longer have to share the same cramped bedroom space.

None of these things mattered to Bridgette though. The thought of leaving her best friend, Sara, behind felt like a hand had seized Bridgette's heart and squeezed the life out of it. Bridgette grieved as if she were in mourning, but the heartache she experienced felt much worse than when her pet hamster died. Her only recourse was to spill her tears into her pillow in order to lessen her suffering.

Through the sounds of her own sniffles and cries, Bridgette heard a knock on her bedroom door. "Bridgette," said her father in a soft comforting voice. "Sweetheart, I'm coming in."

The door creaked open, and her father entered the room. Bridgette's head was buried in her tear-soaked pillow, but she could hear the crackle of the wooden floorboards as her father approached. He sat beside her on the squeaky bed and gently rubbed her back with the palm of his hand. "You understand, don't you? This is the break we've been waiting for all our lives. We'll finally get a chance to escape from this rundown neighborhood and be able to live the life we were meant to live."

Bridgette muttered something, but her words were muffled by her pillow. Her father recognized only one word: Sara.

"Don't worry about not getting to see Sara," said her father. "You'll be able to visit her, and she can visit you too. We can also get you a computer so the two of you can talk for hours online, and you can use my phone to text her."

Bridgette rolled over. "It's not the same, Dad."

"I know, Sweetheart, but it's going to have to do."

Bridgette smothered her face back into her pillow to hide the new tears caused by her father's stabbing words. Mr. Swanson stood, patted his daughter on the back, and quietly crept out of the room.

Later that evening, Bridgette was awakened by the ring of the telephone. She rolled over and wiped the crud from her eyes caused by her dried tears.

She heard a knock on her door. "It's for you, Bridgette!" called her mother from outside the bedroom door. She opened the door and entered the dark room.

"What time is it?" asked Bridgette with a groggy voice.

"It's seven thirty," replied her mom while handing Bridgette the telephone. "It's Sara." Mrs. Swanson walked back out of the room and closed the door behind her.

Bridgette explained the bad news to Sara. She told her about texting each other and Facebooking, pretending that it would be fun, but Sara was not excited. Instead, she began to weep.

"It's not fair," cried Sara. "Best friends are supposed to stick together."

"We'll still be together," said Bridgette, "just apart."

"It won't be the same." Sara sobbed even more now while the thought of her best friend moving away began to sink in.

"If I didn't believe it was for the best, I would tell my parents, no," explained Bridgette. "But it *is* for the best. It's a chance of a lifetime, and I must take advantage of it for my family and for myself. I can't let my family down. They're depending on me to do the sensible thing."

Bridgette began to feel more at ease as she justified her reasons for leaving. She hadn't realized what her parents were trying to explain to her these past few months until she had just now clarified it for Sara.

"This is one of those lifetime decisions that is best made with your head and not your heart," said Bridgette.

"I suppose you're right, as usual," sniveled Sara. "When are you leaving?"

"Well, my parents have always said they would be ready to leave in two weeks whenever they found out."

4

"Okay, for the next two weeks we will spend all of our time together," commanded Sara.

"It's a deal," agreed Bridgette. "We'll be inseparable. Best friends till the end."

Chapter 2

The next two weeks flew by like a gust of wind. Sara and Bridgette spent as much time as possible together. But now the time had finally come to say good-bye.

The final morning was dismal. Most of the packing had been done the night before so the Swansons could get an early start. The sun hadn't cut through the clouds yet, and there was dew still clinging to the ground.

Bridgette lugged the last box into the huge moving truck while Sara sadly dragged her feet behind her.

"Well, that's the last of it," grunted Bridgette while she plopped the box into the back of the moving truck.

"Are you sure?" asked Sara. "Maybe you should take one more look, just in case."

"I'm sure," said Bridgette.

Though it was a depressing time for the girls, it didn't stop the birds from chirping in the apple trees in the surrounding yards.

The two girls stood next to the yellow truck feeling awkward. They had never had to say good-bye to a close friend before. They watched Tommy and one of his friends chase each other around the apartment building in the wet grass.

"Tommy sure is taking it well," said Sara.

"He's still too young to realize what's really going on. Once he's in the truck, and he sees places he's never seen before, it'll probably hit him like a ton of bricks - that he's never coming back."

"I thought you said you'd be back to visit," whined Sara.

"You know what I mean, never coming back to live here again," explained Bridgette. She cupped her hands around her mouth and yelled. "Tommy, it's time to go!"

Like an obedient dog, Tommy raced to the truck and hopped inside through the passenger door where his parents were already patiently waiting.

6

"Well, I guess this is it," said Bridgette.

"I guess so," cried Sara while tears began to stream down her cheeks. They quickly embraced in order to hide each other's tears. Sara tried to remind Bridgette to call her, but the lump in her throat prevented her from uttering any more words.

Bridgette desperately wanted to tell Sara she wouldn't forget to call her, but she too was speechless.

Clouds were beginning to dissolve and separate, and the first ray of sunlight beamed down on Bridgette's forehead.

The honk of the horn by Bridgette's father alarmed the girls causing them to release their grip. They hastily turned away from each other to conceal their teary-eyed faces. Bridgette climbed into the truck and slammed the door shut. Startled, Sara jumped as if the door to Bridgette's life had just been closed forever. Sara wiped the tears from her eyes with her t-shirt and spun around just in time to see Bridgette's face pressed up against the side window. She'll never forget those bloodshot eyes and the way they gazed upon her in anguish while the truck hauled her best friend away from her down the driveway and out of sight.

Chapter 3

The trip lasted two days because the Swansons had decided to stay the night in Bakersfield, California. Besides, if they had driven straight there, it would have taken them almost twenty-two hours of constant driving.

The large yellow rental truck finally pulled into an upper middle class neighborhood. The land was very level. Everything in sight was a sandy color, including the houses. The neighborhood had been built in the desert but was now a section of the city. The streets were immaculate and neatly paved. Solid white sidewalks lined both sides of the roadway.

"Are you sure we're in the right neighborhood, Dad?" asked Bridgette.

"Yep, in fact, there's our new home right there." Mr. Swanson pointed at a house similar in shape and color as the rest of the homes on the street.

"It's so beautiful!" exclaimed Bridgette. "Wait, where's the grass?"

"Too expensive and a waste of water," replied her dad.

The house was in the shape of an "L." It contained only one story but was big enough for a family of four to live comfortably. The outside walls were painted the same color as the desert sand. The house looked newly constructed. In fact, the entire neighborhood appeared to be no more than two years old.

The truck sputtered into the driveway and came to a halt. Tommy and Bridgette leapt out and chased each other around the perimeter of their new home. They sped through the sandy colored gravel in their huge backyard. Too wrapped up in the chase, Bridgette almost collided with a boy her age as she rounded the corner. Startled, she skidded across the rocks, catching herself with her hands as she slid to the ground. Just then she noticed how hot it was because she could feel the perspiration beginning to form from the short chase.

"Here, let me help you up," offered the blond haired boy with an extended arm. Bridgette clasped onto his hand firmly while he pulled her up to her feet.

As she stood, he gave her a quick look over. Her hair was dark brown, straight, and extended beyond her shoulders. She was a couple of inches shorter than he was. She wasn't unpleasant to look at, kind of cute in her own way. When she smiled, he noticed she looked even better.

"Who are you?" asked Bridgette. She brushed the dirt from her brown shorts.

"Apparently, I'm your neighbor. My name is George, but my friends call me Whiz."

"Why do they call you that?" asked Bridgette while she studied him.

His shiny, bleached blond hair was cut tightly above his ears. He wore it combed to the side with a pound of hair product to keep it glued that way. He was slender but did not look like the athletic type. He wore a pair of white shorts and a red t-shirt with a pocket that held his calculator.

"Because I'm a whiz at everything. I know all there is to know about anything and everything under the sun."

"Oh really," said Bridgette, "well, what do you know about bragging?"

"Hey, you asked the question, and I answered it truthfully," he said with an irritated tone. "What's your name?"

"My name is Bridgette, but my friends call me uh......... Bridge."

Why couldn't I have thought of something cooler, thought Bridgette.

"So are you going to the Future School too?" asked George.

"No, I'll be attending the Las Vegas School of Excellence next week," replied Bridgette proudly.

"That's the same place, you rookie," said George snobbishly. "Don't let anyone hear you call it that, if you don't want to get teased."

"Thanks for the tip," said Bridgette. "How long have you been going there?"

"Oh, this is my first year also," replied George. "I've just been here a while, so I've had a chance to learn the ropes."

"I guess that would make you a rookie as well," said Bridgette smartly.

"Yeah, whatever.

"Hey, how much do you have to pay for rent? The Future School wanted me so badly, they're springing for half of our rent. Pretty impressive, huh?"

"That *is* impressive," replied Bridgette. "I'm not sure about our rent. My father is handling all the finances."

Bridgette *did* know, however, that the Future School was paying all of their rent, as well as providing a car for her parents to drive to and from work. They even provided jobs for them at a general elementary school down the road. Her mother would be a third grade teacher, and her father would be the head custodian. Bridgette didn't want to reveal too much about herself just yet.

"It sounds like they really wanted you to attend their school," said Bridgette. "You really *must* be a whiz."

"If you ever need any help, just come see me," said George confidently. "I'm used to it."

"I'll keep that in mind," said Bridgette. "Hey, is it always so hot here?"

"They don't call it the desert for nothing," replied George.

"Bridgette!" hollered Tommy from the other side of the house.

"Well, I've got to go and help my parents unload the truck. I'll talk to you later."

"I'll be here," said George.

While she walked back to the front of the house, she hoped she would discover the rest of the kids in the area were just as nice as George, even if he *did* seem to be a bragger.

What a nice bragger, thought Bridgette. *Totally acceptable. He'll make a good friend.*

Chapter 4

By the time the Swansons had unloaded the truck and unpacked their boxes, it was dinner time. They were just about to pile into the truck to search for an affordable restaurant when a long black limousine pulled into the driveway blocking their exit. A pretty woman with short black hair wearing a navy blue business suit stepped out of the back door. She clip clopped in her blue high heels toward Mr. and Mrs. Swanson with her arm outstretched. "Hello, you must be the Swansons."

"That's right," said Mr. Swanson while shaking the woman's hand. "And you would be…?"

"I'm Ms. Leadbetter. I am the...principal, if you will, at the Las Vegas School of Excellence. I'm the one responsible for making all the accommodations for you and your family. We are very excited to have your daughter attending our school." She reached out and lifted Bridgette's chin with her hand. "This must be the little darling."

"Pleased to meet you," said Bridgette, offering a shaky hand.

While they shook hands, Bridgette couldn't help but notice the firmness of the woman's grip. She gazed into the woman's eyes and shivered. There was an eerie quality about this woman that Bridgette couldn't quite put her finger on. Was it her crooked smile? Perhaps it was the twitch of her nose. Maybe it was the way in which her eyes seemed to laugh wickedly as if she knew something that she did not. Whatever it was, Bridgette trembled inside.

"Yes, well, would someone like to help me carry this new computer into your house?" asked Ms. Leadbetter.

"Sure," volunteered Mr. Swanson.

The two of them carried two separate boxes into the house while Tommy, Bridgette, and their mother, stood outside near the moving truck.

11

The sun had already traveled across most of the sky, and it was still awfully hot, even with the strong gusts of wind that felt more like the hot air from a heater.

"Something's not right about her, Mom," said Bridgette nervously.

"What do you mean?" asked her mother. "She seems like a nice lady. And look at all the trouble she's gone through for us."

"She still gives me the creeps," said Bridgette rudely.

"Bridgette!" scolded her mother, "Where is the loving daughter we all know and love? I don't want to hear you talking that way. I raised you better than that."

"I'm sorry, Mom."

"Here comes Daddy and Creepy," said Tommy with a devilish grin on his face.

"Don't you start too," warned their mother.

Ms. Leadbetter and Mr. Swanson walked back toward the limousine carrying on a pleasant conversation. Mr. Swanson was dabbing his forehead with a red handkerchief.

Ms. Leadbetter, with a twinkle in her eyes, glanced at Bridgette just before she climbed back into the expensive car. "I'll see you at school next week." She flashed that crooked smile again. The door slammed before Bridgette could respond. The chauffeur, who hid behind dark tinted windows, pulled the limousine out of the driveway and drove out of the neighborhood.

"Good news, everyone!" shouted Mr. Swanson. "A new car will be transported here tomorrow for us to use as long as we're here. Also, Ms. Leadbetter told me to take us to this restaurant down the street where we can eat for free. Can you believe it? Bridgette, you must be their star pupil." Mr. Swanson gave his daughter an enormous hug, lifting her off the ground.

Bridgette felt as if the weight of the world was resting upon her shoulders. It was unjust that a twelve-year-old girl or boy experience this amount of pressure. No kid should have to make important life altering decisions. Yet, Bridgette found herself feeling obligated to perform at higher standards than she had ever achieved in the past. She burdened herself constantly with "what if" questions, such as, what if I fail? What if I do not meet the school's expectations? What if I cannot do above average work?

On the other hand, Bridgette also concerned herself with questions, like what if I *do* succeed? What will be expected of me? What does the school want with my success?

"Bridgette, she's talking to you," repeated her mother.

"Huh?" replied Bridgette, snapping out of her daydream. She gazed upward at the waitress, who was smiling at her, waiting patiently to take her order. "Oh, I'll just have what my mom is having."

Chapter 5

Bridgette awoke early Monday morning in order to allow herself ample time to prepare her body and mind for school. She decided it would be a pink day, wearing a pink skirt and a pink top.

The entire family climbed into their new bright blue Cadillac. They began their trip of what was going to become a morning routine. They would drop off Bridgette at the Future School first and then continue on to their own school where Tommy attended. Everything worked out perfectly.

"Have a good day, Sweetheart!" hollered Bridgette's father from the car while she walked toward the colossal school building.

Bridgette spun around with her new book bag hanging over one shoulder, blocked the sun with one hand and waved with the other. She noticed George climbing out of an old Cutlass, so she decided to wait for him. Sure, he was kind of snobby, but she tried to see the best in people. Plus she was all by herself. She didn't enjoy feeling like such a loner on the first day of school.

"Decided to take me up on my offer, I see," said George arrogantly.

George was wearing jeans and a blue blazer, and when Bridgette looked down, she noticed he was wearing sneakers as well. "Just thought you might like some company," she replied.

"Walk with me. I'll show you around," said George. "I've done my research on this building already. I've got the classrooms memorized. Did you know we have to change classrooms here just like the high school kids do? Let's see, first of all, we need to go to the main office to receive our schedules."

"Of course," said Bridgette. "We can't go to class without a schedule."

"Just stick with me," George said confidently. "I wouldn't steer you wrong."

The two new students walked up to the receptionist in the office.

"May I help you?" asked the kind lady from behind the tall counter. The elderly woman walked over and looked at them through her old fashioned framed glasses. Her gray hair was pinned up in the back, exposing the pencil that was lodged behind one ear.

"We would like our schedules," said George with conviction.

"I'm sorry, but you'll need to go to the gymnasium along with the rest of the new students," replied the lady. "Follow the signs. They'll direct you where to go."

"How did you know we were new?" asked George.

"Because if you weren't new, you wouldn't be asking us for your schedules."

"Okay, thanks," replied George.

George turned and glanced at Bridgette while they walked down the crowded hallway.

"They must have changed their procedures," said George sheepishly.

"I'm sure that's it," said Bridgette, holding back her laughter.

They walked into the packed gymnasium. Lines were everywhere. Big signs were posted with letters based on students' last names.

"I'll get in my line while you get in yours," suggested George.

"Sure," agreed Bridgette. "Let's meet back here at the entrance once we get our classes."

After receiving their schedules, George and Bridgette compared classes. They had one class in common at the same time and place. The class was named "Mind over Matter."

"I guess I'll see you in fourth period," said George.

"Yeah, I guess so," responded Bridgette nervously.

George walked away leaving Bridgette alone with thoughts of loneliness.

Suddenly, the school bell rang, and students dispersed along different paths and into opened doors. Squeaky shoe noises could be heard up and down the hallway. Now Bridgette was utterly alone. Uneasily, she walked toward the direction she guessed her first classroom to be. While she wandered aimlessly searching for her math class, she heard an all too familiar clip clopping sound coming up quickly from behind her, causing a chill to engulf her body as if she had just stepped into a giant ice box.

"Bridgette!" called Ms. Leadbetter, her crisp voice echoing mystically down the hallway. "Can I help you find your class?"

Bridgette shut her eyes calmly and took a deep breath. She felt uneasy having to talk to the peculiar principal all alone. Replacing her disappointed frown with a smile, she spun around and presented to Ms. Leadbetter her patented pleased-to-see-you look.

"Yes, I would appreciate some guidance," said Bridgette attempting to speak as proper as possible. "I can't seem to locate any of the room numbers."

"Somehow I had a feeling you might say that," said Ms. Leadbetter confidently.

"How did you know what I would say?" asked Bridgette.

"It's a common question asked around here," explained Ms. Leadbetter. "Did you think I could read your mind or something?"

"Oh, uh…no, not at all," replied Bridgette, feeling relieved that there was a logical explanation to Ms. Leadbetter's presumption.

"Your class is three more doors down on the right," said Ms. Leadbetter.

"Thank you so much," said Bridgette cheerfully.

Ms. Leadbetter isn't such a wicked lady after all, thought Bridgette.

She continued down the hallway and glanced into the other two rooms while she passed and observed each math teacher showing students of all ages how to solve problems. Just as she reached her classroom, it struck her.

How did Ms. Leadbetter know which math class I would be attending?

The tiny hairs on her arms stood on end while that creepy sensation snuck up on her again. She scurried into the silent roomful of students like a frightened mouse and plopped herself down at an empty desk near the door.

Chapter 6

The bell sounded, and Bridgette stood with her loaded book bag strapped over her shoulder, barging out of her third period English class. She trudged down the endless hallway feeling the weight of her backpack becoming heavier with each grueling step. Once again she had no clue as to where she was heading. Barely managing to keep her balance while traversing the busy halls, she survived the trampling of the stampede of bigger and older students roaming to their next class. Not noticing the footsteps this time because of all the commotion, Bridgette was startled when she heard the shrill voice of Ms. Leadbetter coming from behind her only a few feet away.

"Bridgette! Turn around Darling! Your next class is this way!"

She's doing it again, thought Bridgette. *How does she know what my next class is?*

"What *is* my next class?" asked Bridgette innocently, pretending she didn't know.

"It's Mind over Matter, of course," replied Ms. Leadbetter. "Where's your schedule?"

Now Bridgette was really beginning to grow uneasy.

How does she know what class I have next? She had better have a good explanation for this one, thought Bridgette.

"How do you know which class I have next?" she asked the principal.

"Well, Darling, I'd tell you it was magic, but it's not. You just so happen to be in my classroom this period. I'm a teacher also. I teach Mind over Matter. It's an extraordinary class. Come on, let's walk faster. We don't want to be late for our first session."

The sooner the better, thought Bridgette. *This lady is giving me the willies. At least George will be there.*

While Bridgette and Ms. Leadbetter entered the noisy classroom, the small group of frightened children scampered quickly

18

back to their desks. Each of them gazed solemnly at their pretty, but wicked, teacher. Nobody seemed to notice Bridgette when she took her seat in the back of the room. They dared not remove their eyes from Ms. Leadbetter. They too felt the unearthliness surrounding the eccentric woman.

"Good morning, class!" shouted Ms. Leadbetter with a sharp tone like she expected a response. And she received one too.

"Good morning, Ms. Leadbetter!" repeated the chorus of voices from the small classroom. There were only eight students in all. George and Bridgette comprised one-fourth of the small population of the room. Four boys and four girls stared intensely at their new teacher.

Ms. Leadbetter grinned exposing her gums and top canine teeth, which protruded abnormally from her mouth, but only when she smiled.

The kids reared back in their seats not expecting to see a mouthful of fangs.

She walked to the front of the room and stood behind a podium which hid the lower half of her body. "You are not my first class of students," she said, "so therefore, I will most likely forget most of you, unless, of course, you impress me. Each and every one of you are special, or you would not be here. I don't mean the kind of special like your parents tell you either. I mean you have raw talent and the potential to harness this talent into something beyond your wildest dreams. I can tell by the expressions on your faces that you're intrigued. Let me give you a small demonstration of what I'm talking about. What I'm about to do may startle you. Do not be afraid. It is not a trick."

Ms. Leadbetter spun around and stared angrily at the chalkboard where a colorful paper map of the United States stretched downward from a long rod. Suddenly, the map began to tremble. It shook violently against the board until finally it rolled itself up with a loud ruffling noise. The students jerked in their seats. They each heard the sound of their own hearts palpitating through their chests. Their heads began twitching in all directions. If just one of them could muster up enough courage to stand and race out of the room, they would all follow. But no one did.

Sensing the fear in the room, Ms. Leadbetter said, "I know you are feeling scared right now, but don't be. In time you will be able to do the same. And this is just the beginning. It will require a lot of patience and concentration, but I have a feeling most of you will perform well. Of course, some of you will not make the cut. Sorry, but the law of averages says that a few of you will fail this class miserably."

This class is going to be cool, thought Bridgette. She smiled and listened even more to see if there was a catch or something that would prevent them from obtaining the ability.

A security guard wearing a blue and white uniform opened the door and stepped inside the classroom. He was wearing a black cap. He stood next to the door with a taser holstered at his side.

The students all gazed at him, noticing the black taser gun especially.

"With that in mind," said Ms. Leadbetter in a calmer voice, "I want you to read this release form that was signed by your parents." She handed a sheet of paper to each student and returned to the podium. "These forms give us the right to inject you with an experimental drug, which will enhance your ability to use the power of your minds. Don't worry, it's not harmful. I have used it myself. Your parents would not have signed the forms if they thought it would be harmful to you in any way."

George raised his hand.

"Yes, George," answered Ms. Leadbetter.

"Um, it says here that you and the school are not responsible if I were to die or become incapacitated from any adverse effects of the drug. My parents would never have signed something like this."

"What is the name signed at the bottom of the page?" asked Ms. Leadbetter with confidence.

"Well, it's obviously my mom's name, but-"

"But what? Are you telling me you are having second thoughts about going to our illustrious school? Because if so, then we can just bring in one of the many students who are just *dying* to take your place."

George closed his mouth and stared at his mom's signature while shaking his head.

The door opened again, and a woman dressed in a white nurse's uniform strolled into the room pushing a metal cart that contained syringes and small bottles of liquid, which contained the experimental drug. The security guard took his position again at the door.

"I have asked Nurse Meyers to assist me with the brain enhancing liquid," said Ms. Leadbetter. "Please roll up the sleeve of your right arm. The good news is that this will be your one and only shot."

The students' faces grew pale. They looked nauseous. They were totally unprepared to experience pain on their first day of school. A couple looked at the door like they might try to make a run for it, but the security guard was there, waving at them.

One by one, the inoculation was given.

When it was Bridgette's turn, she clenched her teeth together and turned her head away from Nurse Meyers. She felt the piercing poke of the stinging needle and grimaced. When it was over, Bridgette examined her arm to discover a small round bandage on the sore spot. Then she smiled, eager to get started.

George tried to protest during his turn. "This doesn't look like my mother's signature," he complained. "I'm not so sure my parents have agreed to this. They would have mentioned something to me."

His objection was ignored. It only caused Ms. Leadbetter to roll up his sleeve herself and hold his arm while the nurse stabbed the needle into it.

After the last shot was given, the nurse and the security guard left, and Ms. Leadbetter marched back to the front of the room behind the podium. "Okay, we still have twenty quality minutes to begin our first lesson. The drug will take effect immediately, so we don't need a waiting period. This drug will remain in your bodies for the rest of your lives. Here's what I want you to do: take one of these brand new pencils and place it on the top of your desk." She held a typical yellow pencil in the air.

Everyone retrieved a pencil from the podium and obediently followed the order.

"Good. Now this is where the patience and concentration part comes in. I want all of you to clear your minds of all thoughts and ideas for the moment. Once your mind is clear, I want you to stare at your pencil and concentrate as hard as you can. Try to move the pencil with your eyes while at the same time, thinking about the pencil moving. Nobody, and I mean nobody, not even I have been successful in doing this on the very first day. Don't get frustrated. You'll all be able to do this now that you have the brain serum pulsing through your veins."

Bridgette raised her hand and asked, "How long did it take you?"

Ms. Leadbetter glared at her and then relaxed her face. "Bridgette, darling, nobody called on you, and that's none of your business."

Bridgette frowned while she sank down into her chair, looking as small as Ms. Leadbetter made her feel.

Who does she think she is? thought Bridgette.

Maybe it was the effect of the medicine or possibly just a daydream, but Bridgette seemed to be in a daze. While she was, she could hear Ms. Leadbetter in the background.

"Remember, I am not just your teacher; I am also the principal here at this school. Let's not forget that. Nothing happens here without my approval, and right now I don't approve of the way some of you are thinking. I can hear your thoughts, and frankly, I don't care if you don't like me. I'm not here to be your friend."

Ms. Leadbetter struck Bridgette's desk with a pointing stick. The loud noise caused the whole room to jump.

"Snap out of it, Bridgette! Concentrate, or you'll ruin the timing of the experiment."

Bridgette sat up straight and stared at her pencil with her eyebrows furrowed.

Ms. Leadbetter walked past her and stared at each child's pencil.

Bridgette glared at her pencil like she hated it, and that's when it happened. It started vibrating, shaking back and forth. Bridgette's eyes grew wide.

George, who was sitting right next to her, could hear the slight movement of her pencil. He lost his focus and turned his head. His mouth dropped open.

Bridgette turned her head to see where Ms. Leadbetter was patrolling the room. Her back was to her. She looked back at her pencil again…then back at Ms. Leadbetter…then back at her pencil. Back and forth she pivoted her head like she was working up her anger or something. Finally with a jerk of her head one last time, she willed her pencil to fly across the room. It twirled in the air like a baton until it struck Ms. Leadbetter in the back.

Bridgette noticed from the corner of her eye that George had witnessed it all. Somehow she knew he was going to toss her his pencil. She caught it in midair just in time to place it gently on her desk before Ms. Leadbetter turned around to look for her assailant.

Ms. Leadbetter turned directly toward Bridgette, expecting that it would have been her who threw the pencil, but she saw Bridgette's pencil sitting on top of her desk, motionless.

Slowly and deliberately, George pulled another pencil from his pocket and placed it carefully on his desk without Ms. Leadbetter noticing.

"Who just hit me with a pencil?"

Everybody thought the same thing: *It wasn't me.*

Ms. Leadbetter looked each student in the eyes, just waiting for someone to blink. After checking everyone she stopped and said, "Hmm, that's odd. I can't figure out who did it, at least not yet. It appears we have a trickster in our midst."

The next fifteen minutes passed, and nobody else succeeded in persuading a pencil to move. The bell rang, and everybody let out a big sigh as if they had been holding their breath.

"That's okay," said Ms. Leadbetter. "We'll continue this tomorrow; however, I must issue one warning. Do not, I repeat, *do not* continue this lesson at home. It is imperative that you perform this task only in this classroom. Timing has a lot to do with what we are doing here. I need to know exactly how long it takes you before you are able to move your pencils with your minds. Trying to do this at home will throw off the results, and we cannot afford to be inaccurate with our findings. Go now, and I'll see you tomorrow."

The students filed out of the room, pushing and shoving each other. While they did, Ms. Leadbetter stood at the door and watched them with her arms folded across her chest. She peered down at each student with an "I'm-watching-you" sort of look.

Bridgette and George were the last ones to leave. Bridgette went first and did her best to give Ms. Leadbetter the friendly version of the "I'm-watching-you-too" look back.

When George tried to pass, Ms. Leadbetter held out her arm and said, "Wait!"

George gulped.

"Let me see your pencil."

George, still clutching his pencil after he had picked it up to leave, held it up for her to see.

Ms. Leadbetter plucked the yellow pencil from his hand and placed her thumb on the pointed end. A vein popped out of her forehead, and her hand shook until her thumb pressed down hard enough to get punctured by the sharpened tip. A drop of blood squeezed out.

George swallowed again and said, "What are you doing to my pencil?"

Ms. Leadbetter grinned. "You're right about one thing; it is *your* pencil. What I want to know is: WHERE IS *MY* PENCIL! Where is the pencil I gave you earlier, the one that had *not* been sharpened?"

Bridgette, already standing in the hallway waiting for George, started to come back into the classroom, but Ms. Leadbetter pressed her hand with the bloody thumb against Bridgette's blouse, pushed her backwards and said, "Stay out, Bridgette. This doesn't concern you."

Bridgette put one finger in the air, but before she could utter a word, the door slammed in her face. She gazed downward to find Ms. Leadbetter's bloody thumbprint on her beautiful pink blouse.

She turned, and without even looking where she was going, she bumped right into another one of the students in the class who hadn't run off yet.

"Ouch! My arm! Watch where you're going!"

Bridgette regained her balance after awkwardly stumbling backwards. "I'm sorry, I didn't see you. You came out of nowhere."

The girl grabbed her own arm and rubbed it. "Right where we got that stupid shot. How'd you like it if I hit *your* arm where you got *your* shot?"

"I said I was sorry," pleaded Bridgette, "but if that isn't good enough, then here, hit my sore arm back so we'll be even." Bridgette held her arm out for the girl to punch.

"I might be mean, but I'm not that mean," responded the girl. She reached over and slugged Bridgette in her other arm.

Bridgette doubled over and fell to the floor.

"What's wrong?" asked the girl. "I didn't hit you in the same arm you got your shot in."

"Do you think I would have offered you my sore arm? You *did* hit me in the arm I got my shot in."

The girl laughed. "I guess that's what you get for trying to trick me."

Bridgette, with tears in her eyes from the pain, starting chuckling as well. She stood up and held out her hand. "I'm Bridgette."

"You can put your hand down. My name is Janice."

Bridgette had to look up at Janice when they spoke as Janice towered over her. She was slender and kept her short brown hair hanging straight down to her eyebrows covering her forehead.

"You're pretty tall," noticed Bridgette. "How old are you?"

"I'm twelve. How about you?"

"Same," replied Bridgette. "So how did you like the first day of class in "*Mind over Matter*?" She said it like it was a spooky name.

Janice rubbed her arm. "Pretty creepy, right?"

"I'll say," agreed Bridgette. "And did you hear her say how she knew what we were thinking?"

"She never said that," said Janice, looking confused.

"Yes, she said it right before she struck the desk with that pointing stick, remember?"

Janice shook her head. "You're crazy, girl. Ms. Leadbottom was just walking around the room. I remember because I watched her sneak up on you just before she hit the desk."

Bridgette laughed. "Leadbottom?"

"I'm sure she's been called worse."

"Hmm, well, I guess it's possible I fell asleep and dreamt it," said Bridgette. "She did startle me when she hit the desk with that stick. I just don't remember being tired."

"I'd like to hit *her* with that stick," said Janice.

"Aren't we the violent one?" said Bridgett rhetorically.

"You just noticed?" said Janice.

"Well, it's lunch time now," said Bridgette, trying to change the subject. "How would you like to go beat up some food, squirt some catsup on it for the bloody effect, and then eat it?"

Janice turned her head to the side and looked at Bridgette strangely. "You are one weird chick, but who am I to judge? I've got my own issues."

"And what might those be?" inquired Bridgette.

Janice put her face right in front of Bridgette until their noses almost touched and then snarled. "I thought we just got through discussing this. I've got an anger problem."

"Duly noted," squeaked Bridgette while she backed her face away. Then her eyes widened. "Hey, there's George. I'm sure he knows the way to the cafeteria. George! George! Help! I mean, help us find the cafeteria."

George closed the classroom door behind him and swaggered up to the two girls. "Did I hear someone call for help? You've come to the right guy. Remember, I told you to call me Whiz. Now, I know where everything is around here. In this case, we just need to follow our noses." He spun ninety degrees, sniffed, and said, "This way."

"So, what happened?" asked Bridgette. "Did she stab you with that pencil?" She tried to roll up his sleeve to search for the wound.

"Very funny, Bridge. Let's just say I won't be throwing pencils at *her* anymore." He winked.

"You've got guts, man," said Janice. "I admire that."

"Thanks." George was beaming. He held out his hand. "I'm George, also known as Whiz. And you are…?"

Janice stared at his hand and then said, "Janice."

George dropped his hand and said, "Nice to meet you."

She nodded.

The unlikely trio walked together toward the cafeteria. Simultaneously, George tried to put one arm around each of the girls, but they both shrugged him off. Then Janice slugged him in the shoulder.

Chapter 7

The cafeteria was abuzz with kids coming and going, sitting and standing, talking and laughing. Bridgette grabbed three trays and handed one to George.

"Thank you," said George.

She handed another one to Janice.

Janice jerked the tray from Bridgette's hand. "Yeah, what he said."

They each paid for a burger, fries, and a soft drink and then started looking for a place to sit. The eating area was packed.

They wandered through an ocean of tables searching aimlessly until the tallest of the three, Janice, said, "Wait, I see one." She led them toward the middle of the room to a round table that would fit six people comfortably. A group of girls arrived at the same time, three of them. Bridgette and one of the other girls rushed to a chair, as if whoever sat down first would be the winner of the table. Their trays collided together, shuffling the food around on Bridgette's plate, spilling a few French fries onto the table.

One of the girls still standing, obviously the leader of the three, snarled, "Well, I guess this table is already taken. You maggots will have to find another place to sit."

"*All right*," sang Janice, seemingly impressed, "finally, someone who speaks my language." She set down her tray and walked up to the girl and faced her like she did Bridgette earlier. Janice was taller and more menacing. She stared angrily down at the girl.

The girl looked to be about thirteen, long blonde hair in a ponytail, blue eyes, and dressed in designer clothing. Though she tried to hide it, she gulped while she turned toward her other friend that hadn't sat down yet. "Can you believe this, Cathy? She thinks we're in an alley or something."

Cathy chuckled, causing the red freckles on her face to shift back and forth. "As *if*!" She twirled her long red hair in her fingers.

The girl who had sat down said, "Are you sure she's not a dude?" The three girls laughed in unison.

Janice took a step toward the girl sitting down and said, "You're gonna regret ever-"

"Regret what?" grunted a loud voice from behind her. A hand clutched onto Janice's shoulder preventing her from charging toward the other girl.

Janice turned around and faced her attacker. This girl was at least 17 and much taller than her...meaner looking too if it were possible. She was a thickly built tower. Her hair was dark brown, wrapped up in a red bandana. She was standing with two of her friends around the same size. Gazing down at Janice without flinching, she said, "Is everything okay here, sis?"

The girl sitting down said, "It is now. Looks like some newbies hadn't been told that this is *our* table."

Bridgette and Janice both looked at George.

George's face turned beet red. "What? I can't get into any trouble. I'm here on a scholarship."

"That explains your wardrobe," jabbed Cathy. "And I thought you were just fashion-challenged."

Janice realized she was outmatched, but she knew how to back away in style. "I'm gonna let you guys have this table... today. Enjoy your diet soda and laxatives."

Bridgette rose from her seat and followed George and Janice away from the table. Another table opened up about thirty feet away. They scurried over to it and sat down.

Janice looked angry, but then again, she always looked angry.

Bridgette said, "It's okay, Janice. We were outnumbered, and three of them were much older than us."

"Don't try to cheer me up," snarled Janice. "It doesn't work. You're just wasting your breath."

Bridgette glanced at the table of girls and said, "Those girls are gonna get what's coming to them." She clenched her teeth and focused on their food trays which only carried sodas with straws. Her body stiffened, and she jerked her head to the right. When she did, each of the girls' trays flew off the table, spilling their drinks all over the place. The girls scooted their chairs away from the table all at once, making a spectacle of themselves. Bridgette smiled and then placed her hand over her lips to conceal her amusement.

George pointed. "Hey, look! They just spilled their drinks." He peeked over at Bridgette just in time to see her stop smiling at the incident. "Hey, did you-"

"Pass me the salt, George." She winked at him and shook her head.

Janice glanced at the other table, and her frown straightened out a bit. She didn't smile, but for an instant, she didn't appear to be upset. By the time Bridgette looked at her, she had changed back to her usual mean-looking self.

Satisfied that no one except George saw what she had done and, at the same time, amazed with her new ability, Bridgette smiled and then took a big bite of her hamburger.

Chapter 8

Bridgette's mom opened the white oven door with one of those funny looking padded mitts with the giant thumb. The wave of heat blew into the dining room like a soft warm breeze. Accompanying the flow of cozy air was the mouth-watering aroma of Rosemary baked chicken.

"It smells delicious, honey," said Mr. Swanson, sitting at the rectangular dining room table with Bridgette.

Tommy finished setting the silverware on the table next to the empty plates and took his seat by his sister. He picked up his knife and fork in each hand and began pounding them on the table as he chanted. "I want food. I want food. I want food."

"Patience is a virtue, Tommy," said Bridgette.

"Patients are in the hospital," Tommy replied smartly.

"Dad," whined Bridgette.

"Tommy, sit there and wait for your mother to serve you," commanded their father.

"Sorry, Daddy," Tommy apologized.

Tommy was only seven years old, but he was a wise guy. He didn't have Bridgette's remarkable intelligence. However, he did resemble Bridgette, in a manner of speaking. He had her brown eyes and dark hair color. There was no mistaking them for brother and sister.

Mrs. Swanson placed the chicken in the center of the table next to the bowls of potatoes and green beans and sat down. "So how was your first day of school, you two?" she asked, staring directly at Bridgette.

Bridgette began, "Well-"

"I learned about dinosaurs!" blurted out Tommy.

Their mom looked back at Tommy. "That's nice, dear." She turned back to Bridgette. "What about you, Bridgette? Did you learn about anything interesting today?"

"I have this really strange class called "Mind over Matter," replied Bridgette. "And you'll never guess who my teacher is. It's Ms. Leadbetter. Even the kids at school think she's creepy."

"Bridgette, what did I tell you about that?" scolded her mother with a harsh voice.

31

"Sorry, Mom."

Lost in thought about Bridgette's last statement, Mr. Swanson suddenly asked, "What's so strange about the class?"

"I don't know for sure, Dad," responded Bridgette while pulling her fork away from her mouth. "All I know is that she's got us trying to move our pencils on our desks by using our minds.

"Oh, yeah, why didn't you guys tell me I was going to get a shot?"

"Shot? What shot?" asked her mother with a concerned voice.

"Everyone received an injection of some sort of brain serum today." Bridgette pulled up her shirt sleeve to expose the little round bandage.

"This is outrageous!" shouted Mr. Swanson, dropping his fork on his plate. "Nobody told us anything about getting shots."

"Don't get too excited, dear," said Mrs. Swanson calmly. "It's not good for your digestion. I'm sure it was just some sort of vaccine for the measles or something."

"Measles," giggled Tommy. He began placing the little seeds from his green beans on the sculpture of a dinosaur that he molded from his mashed potatoes.

"Moving pencils with their brains?" Mr. Swanson questioned. "What kind of nonsense is that?"

"It's not nonsense, Daddy," cried Bridgette.

"Bridgette, you're only 12 years old," said her father. Veins were beginning to pulse on his forehead. "I don't think you're old enough to make that call."

Bridgette frowned, and then she stared intensely at the mushy prehistoric creature on Tommy's plate. Looking as if she were in a trance, her eyes began to twitch. The head of the dinosaur lifted gently from its white squishy body and floated in the air. Tommy's mouth opened wide in disbelief. Suddenly, the dinosaur drifted between Tommy's lips and disappeared into the back of his mouth.

"Oh my goodness! It's true!" exclaimed Mr. Swanson. "What have they done to you?"

Bridgette's mom put her hand over her mouth.

"Nobody else can do it yet, Dad. I'm the only one. Ms. Leadbetter doesn't know either. She said no one has ever been able to move the pencil on the first day, but *I* did. She didn't see it though. I don't want her to know."

"Why not, honey?" asked her mom.

Tommy gulped down the potatoes and shouted, "More! More!" He threw his fork on the floor and opened his mouth wide while pointing with both hands at the opening.

"I don't trust her," responded Bridgette.

Bridgette's mom looked concerned.

Her dad saw the look on his wife's face and said, "Well, honey, you know how your mother, I mean how *we* feel about giving people the benefit of the doubt: innocent until proven guilty. Let's not be too hasty in our judgment. After all, she's the one who arranged for us to come out here and got us our jobs. It's a great blessing for our family."

"I know, Dad. I want to trust her, but something tells me she's no good."

"Bridgette," said her mother with a tone of warning. "You'll need more proof than that."

Bridgette stared down at her plate. "Sorry."

Her dad clapped his hands together. "Well, I don't think it's a big crime to keep this little secret from her. Let's just wait and see how long it takes for the others to do it." He looked to his wife for approval. She smiled.

"Nobody else knows," said Bridgette, "except George, the boy next door."

"Are you sure that was wise," said her father. "You barely know the boy."

"I didn't tell him. He *saw* me do it."

"Well, do you think he can keep your secret?" asked her dad. "If he tells on you, it could jeopardize our entire future here."

"He doesn't like her either, Dad."

"Bridgette!" yelled her mom.

"Oops," said Bridgette, "I mean, *he* doesn't like her. I'm still making up my mind."

Chapter 9

The bell rang, and everyone focused their attention on Ms. Leadbetter. Only the second day of class and already her students were well-trained. They watched her walk and stand behind the podium where she spent most of her time in the classroom. She looked like she was going to a funeral, dressed in all black, a pair of slacks and a matching blouse.

"Thank you," said Ms. Leadbetter. "Before we begin today's exercise I have an important question to ask all of you. Who can tell me what my specific directions were yesterday before you left my classroom?" All eight timid students sat in their chairs until finally a courageous hand belonging to a red-headed girl shook nervously in the air. "Yes, Karen."

"You said that it was important that we do not practice attempting to move our pencils at home with our minds because you need to know exactly how long it takes us to do it."

"That's exactly right!" shouted Ms. Leadbetter as she clung onto both sides of the podium with her long-nailed fingertips. "Now listen carefully to my next question. Who did not follow those directions, or who knows of anyone who did not follow those directions?"

Silence. No hands.

"Nobody, huh?" said Ms. Leadbetter disappointedly. "Speak now, or pay the consequences."

Bridgette knew she had used the ability once at lunch and once at dinner, but it wasn't trying to move a pencil so she didn't even feel guilty. She also didn't dare think about it in front of Ms. Leadbetter since she thought the woman might be able to read her mind.

Five long seconds passed.

"Okay, now that that's out of the way, I want you to begin willing your pencil to move with your minds. Take your time. We've got all period." She wrote the time on the whiteboard with a black marker. "We'll take a break every 20 minutes."

Bridgette stared at her pencil and relaxed. She had to make sure she didn't accidentally move it since it seemed it was getting easier to move things each time she tried.

She glanced at Janice and George whenever Ms. Leadbetter wasn't watching her. They were staring intensely at their pencils. George even had a drop of sweat sliding down his cheek. She couldn't tell if Janice was trying hard or not because her normal expression was menacing, so it just looked like she was mad at her pencil.

Each twenty minute session was fruitless. Nobody's pencil moved.

After the last session, the bell rang, and Ms. Leadbetter said, "I know you're bored right now, but trust me; this is going to be the most exciting class you've ever had. Just give it a little more time. It took me two full class sessions to move *my* pencil. Don't give up hope. You will all be successful. It's just a matter of time."

The bell rang, and they all filtered out of the classroom. George, Janice, and Bridgette started walking toward the cafeteria.

"I don't know about *you* guys," said George, "but I'm getting tired of staring at a pencil, thinking it's going to move. I feel like an idiot."

"Well, now you feel like you look," replied Janice.

"Seriously, when is something going to happen?" asked George. "I want to know what comes next." He looked at Bridgette. "Who do *you* think is going to be first?"

Bridgette glared at him and replied, "It won't be me."

"Why not?" asked George.

"It seems like they need us for something. I don't want to be their prized guinea pig."

"Well, *I'm* gonna practice tonight," declared George, "*all* night if I have to."

Bridgette's mouth gaped open. "But….that's against the rules. She'll find out."

"How?" George questioned. "Are you going to tell her?"

"Of course not, but seriously, I think she can read minds."

"Well, she can't read *my* mind if I don't think about it," said George as if he knew anything about reading minds.

Janice patted him on the back and said, "Guts, man. You got guts."

Bridgette said, "Guts? More like selective guts. Remember how he wouldn't break the rules about fighting in the cafeteria yesterday? But he's willing to break *this* rule."

"Physical fights are beneath me," responded George. "I fight with my mind. Besides, I'm used to being first. I'm sure I have the most experience in the class with winning. When I'm first tomorrow, I'll be able to move the class forward and see what you're so worried about."

"You're risking your scholarship," warned Bridgette.

"It's not a risk if you can't get caught," replied George.

"Yes, well, ask all the crooks if they thought they'd ever get caught," said Bridgette.

George shook his head. "I'm doing you guys a favor. I got this. Don't worry."

"If you're *really* going to go through with it," said Bridgette, "we need to make sure that none of us even thinks about what you're doing when we're in class tomorrow because Ms. Leadbetter might find out. I don't want anything bad to happen to you, George."

"Don't worry," said George confidently.

They entered the cafeteria, picked up their food from the line, and paid for it at the register. This time they walked to one side of the room, purposely avoiding the table they were forced to give up yesterday. Again, an empty table was difficult to find, but one eventually opened up, and sure enough, just as they were about to sit down, the same group of three girls strolled up to them.

"Don't even *think* about sitting at our table, maggots," said their leader with the blonde ponytail.

"Not you again," groaned Bridgette.

Janice put her tray down and asked, "You got your whole family here today to back you up? Because you're gonna need it."

Their leader turned to one of her friends, the one with long, brown wavy hair. "Maria, where's your sister?"

"Wanda, let's just let 'em have it," said Maria. "I think she and her friends went off campus today for lunch."

Janice stepped toward Wanda and then pushed her shoulder. "Yeah, why don't you do what Mary said?"

Wanda rolled her eyes. "Her name is *Maria*, not *Mary*."

Janice got in her face and gritted her teeth. "Her name is whatever I say it is."

Wanda took a step back and bumped into Cathy. She cleared her throat and said, "Fine, you can have the stinking table, but don't go to sleep tonight if you know what's good for you. And that goes for all *three* of you."

Cathy spoke up. "Wanda, you can't. It's against the rules. You're gonna get us into trouble."

"Can't what?" asked Bridgette.

"None of your business," snapped Wanda. She turned toward Cathy. "I *can*, and I *will*."

"Ha…ha…ha," laughed Janice slowly. "Am I supposed to give you back your table now, Rhonda?"

"It's Wanda. I can't believe-"

"Rhonda!" Janice put a finger up to Wanda's mouth. "Be quiet. We've already gone over this. Your name is whatever I say it is."

"*Whatever.* Sleep well, skanks." Wanda spun around, and her plaid skirt twirled with her. "Let's go, girls."

George sat at the table and finally exhaled, blowing his bangs in the air. "What do you think they're going to do to us when we're sleeping?"

"Not a thing," answered Janice. "They don't even know our addresses."

Bridgette had a strange feeling, however, that Wanda wouldn't need to know where they lived.

Later that night Bridgette lay in her bed, staring at the ceiling. It was just before midnight, and she had tossed and turned for what felt like hours but had only been 40 minutes. Every little sound outside her window made her tremble. It didn't help that it was a windy night as it usually was in Las Vegas. She crawled out of bed at least three times to peek through the curtains. Scanning the area, she saw sinister branches and their shadows clawing at the air but nothing else.

Chapter 10

Bridgette, George, and Janice strolled down the hallway to the cafeteria. The overhead lights were flickering randomly as a stronger than usual windstorm was blowing gusts of air against the building.

"We're supposed to have some pretty strong winds today," said George.

"Duh," said Janice. She cupped her hand around her ear to show him she could hear the wind outside.

George smiled, and so did Bridgette.

They entered the cafeteria and grabbed their trays, the usual routine. Janice spanked George with the back of her tray before getting in line.

They waited for each other to finish paying before searching for a table together. They didn't dare try to find a table alone, not in this place.

Bridgette found a table first. "I see one!" She looked across the cafeteria and noticed Wanda and a few other girls headed toward it as well.

Why are they always after our table? thought Bridgette.

"We'd better run if we're gonna get there in time," announced Bridgette. "Wanda and her *girls* are on the prowl."

They speed-walked toward the table, but it was too late; Cathy had cut them off from another angle.

Wanda slowed her walk and finally stepped up to Bridgette and stopped. Everyone who had been eating in the cafeteria stared at them and froze.

"So, I see you're still trying to steal our table," snarled Wanda. She spoke through gritted teeth. "How many times do I have to tell you this table is mine?"

Bridgette was about to say something, but George spoke first.

"Once was enough," said George cowardly. "I think I see another table over there." He started to walk off until one of Wanda's goons slapped him on the chest and left her hand there.

He looked down at her red fingernails and said, "Nice polish job."

"Shut up, maggot!" screamed the girl.

Janice grabbed the girl's hand and pulled it away from George. "I don't see anybody's big sister here to protect you."

"We're not the ones that need protection," said Wanda. "You do. But you're not gonna find it today."

Janice strode across the floor, nudged Bridgette aside, and walked up to Wanda. "You know, you're pretty funny, but I don't laugh that easily." She grabbed Wanda's shirt with both hands and started to push her backwards. Well, she tried to push her back, but Wanda wasn't budging.

Wanda karate chopped Janice's hands to loosen her grip. Then, with one hand, she clenched Janice's arm and squeezed it like a lemon. Her hand shook violently while she tightened her grip.

Janice's eyes tightened shut until tears trickled from each one. "You're breaking my arm!" she cried.

No one really believed it until a bone cracked causing Janice to scream bloody murder throughout the cafeteria.

Bridgette's eyes bulged at the sight and sound of it all. She panicked and took a step backward. She glared at Wanda and then threw her head to the left, trying to throw Wanda through the air like the trays...like the pencil. Nothing. She gasped.

Wanda gave her a confident look and said, "Your powers or special ability, whatever you want to call it, won't work in here. We own this place, and just to prove it, I'm going to show you. Get ready for the pain because it's real."

Bridgette took a step backward and bumped into a crowd of pushing hands, a mob of people who weren't going to let her run. She was trapped. They shoved her forward.

Bridgette closed her eyes and held out her arms to keep Wanda away. "No! We're sorry! We'll eat somewhere else."

Wanda grabbed onto one of her arms like she had done to Janice. Tightly, she crushed, and she crushed.

George had already been thrown to the floor while people were kicking him in the gut. He covered up his face and tried curling into a ball to protect himself as much as possible.

Janice stood there with a wet face, holding her arm gently.

Bridgette opened one eye and saw Wanda's hand shaking while she tried squeezing the life out of her arm.

Why doesn't it hurt? thought Bridgette.

Wanda stared at Bridgette's arm confusedly. When Bridgette didn't respond to the pressure she was applying to her arm, Wanda released it and amazingly floated up toward the ceiling.

Bridgette followed her with her eyes and wondered, *What kind of powers are they teaching her here?*

Cathy and Maria rose from the ground next. They soared high above the crowded cafeteria. They huddled about twenty feet above Bridgette, and then they started falling fast, heading right for Bridgette, feet first.

Bridgette gasped at the bottoms of the six shoes heading right for her face. She covered her face with her arms, closed her eyes, and screamed, "Noooooooooooo!"

Instantly, she sat up in bed, took a deep breath, and thought about what had just happened in her dream.

So that's what Wicked Wanda meant when she said, 'Don't go to sleep tonight, if you know what's good for you.'

She reached for her cell phone, given to her from the school, and texted George. ARE YOU AWAKE?

Pause.

YES.

WHY? asked Bridgette.

BAD DREAMS.

ABOUT WANDA?

HOW DID YOU KNOW? typed George.

SHE TOLD US NOT TO GO TO SLEEP TONIGHT.

SHE CAN GIVE US NIGHTMARES? typed George.

APPARENTLY, replied Bridgette.

BTW, CAN YOU MOVE THINGS YET?

NOPE, TRIED ALL DAY TOO.
PATIENCE IS A VIRTUE, typed Bridgette.
MAYBE TOMORROW. GOOD NIGHT.
GOOD NIGHT.

Chapter 11

The next day George hitched a ride with Bridgette and her family. It was peaceful in the car. No one had anything to say, at least anything they wanted each other to hear. George looked like he was going to pop, but he kept quiet.

Bridgette's parents dropped George and Bridgette off at the school and drove away. They walked with their backpacks, each over one shoulder, toward the school building, passing students coming and going. They kept to the sidewalk that made a huge rectangle around the bright green grass growing in front of the school, which looked well-groomed and out of place considering most landscapes in the area were decorated with colored gravel.

"Finally!" cried George. "I did it!" He placed his hands on his hips.

"Did what?" asked Bridgette.

"I moved my pencil this morning at breakfast."

"That's great," responded Bridgette. "Are you going to move it again in class today? You know… to be the first one to do it?"

"Well, you were the first," replied George.

"You know what I mean."

"I suppose I should so I can find out what's next. After all, you're all counting on me to go first, right?"

Bridgette wrinkled her forehead. "Uh, sure."

George rubbed his ribs.

"Are you okay?"

"I hope so," said George. "That dream last night seemed pretty real." He pulled up his shirt to look for bruises, but there were none.

Bridgette's eyes lit up. "Were people kicking you in the ribs while you were on the ground?"

"You had the same dream?"

"I think so," answered Bridgette. "They must be pretty strong to bring us all into the same dream. We'll have to ask Janice if she had the dream too."

"Let's find out," said George. "There she is now."

Janice walked up to them carrying her backpack with one arm while her other arm looked to be in a homemade sling made of white bandages.

"Janice," said Bridgette, "did you have a dream last night about Wanda and the cafeteria?"

"I don't know if that was a dream or not," said Janice. She looked down at her arm resting across her stomach, suspended in cloth.

"Wanda broke it with her hand, didn't she?" suggested Bridgette.

"It sure hurts like she did, but I just got back from the doctor, and he said there's nothing wrong with my arm. Everything I described to him sounded like a fracture, but there's no swelling, and the x-rays were negative."

"My ribs hurt also," said George, "and I don't have any bruises or scrapes or anything. But in the dream I was being kicked by a lot of people."

Janice nodded her head at Bridgette. "What about you, Bridgette? They came flying down on your head pretty hard. You were bleeding and everything."

"Really?" said Bridgette. "What happened after that?"

"Don't you know?" asked Janice.

"Actually, I don't because I woke up screaming."

"Yes," agreed Janice, "you were screaming 'Nooooooo!' just before they all three kicked you in the head and knocked you to the floor. When you tried to stand, Wanda threw you back down and told you not to get up until she told you to. Your nose was gushing blood. Then she leaned over you and said, 'Next time you better listen to me when I tell you something at school.'"

"Then what?" asked Bridgette.

"That's all *I* remember," said George.

"Yeah, that's where it all ended," said Janice.

"So we all had the same dream," said Bridgette, thinking aloud.

"And the pain is real," said George, holding onto his ribs. "Well, kinda real. It hurts later, but there's no evidence or marks."

"So now we know what they're learning here at Future School," said Janice. "And if we can wake up before they hurt us, we should be fine."

"Not necessarily," interrupted Bridgette. "Before I woke up, Wanda tried squeezing my arm like she did yours, but I couldn't feel anything, and she looked surprised."

Janice scowled. "So what are you saying? You're untouchable or something?"

"Maybe," replied Bridgette. "It only happened once. Perhaps it was just a fluke."

"I'll bet it has to do with you being able to move your pencil on the first day of class," said George.

"What?" said Janice. She looked at George. "You mean you didn't throw your pencil?" She turned to Bridgette. "It was you? *You* threw it with your *mind*?"

Bridgette glared at George, obviously upset that he had given away her secret. "She made me mad, kind of like what George is doing right now."

George held out his hands. "Please don't hit me with a pencil too."

Bridgette couldn't help but laugh at him.

"Well, since we're spilling the beans this morning," said Bridgette, looking at George, "let's not forget about how you practiced last night *and* this morning until you could move *your* pencil now too."

"Wow!" exclaimed Janice. "I thought *I* was brave and bold, but you two are either the gutsiest people I know, or you're the stupidest. Do you know what Ms. Leadbottom is going to do to you when she finds out?"

"How's she gonna find out?" asked George.

Janice pointed at Bridgette. "Untouchable over here says Ms. Leadbottom can read minds. How long do you think you, and even *I*, can go without thinking about it in class?"

Bridgette glared at George. "And *that's* why we're supposed to keep it a secret. The less people that know, the better."

"But she's our friend now," said George defensively.

"Which is why you shouldn't have told her, *Whiz.*" Bridgette didn't mean it as a compliment when she called him that. "Now, if Ms. Leadbetter finds out about us, she might also find out that Janice knew and was withholding the information."

Bridgette thought for a moment. "Okay, here's what we're gonna do. George, since you were going to move your pencil in class today anyway in order to be the first one, go ahead and do it. Make sure it happens within the first few minutes so she doesn't have time to read our minds. Right after you do it, I'm going to move mine as well. I guess we're about to find out what the next step of our training is going to be. I think we need to speed things along anyway. We need to strengthen our skills to go up against Wanda."

George gulped. "Why do we have to go up against Wanda? Can't we just let them have our table?"

"It's not about the table," said Bridgette. "It's about respect. We may be new here, but we don't have to be treated like it."

Janice held up her hand for Bridgette to slap. "I don't know what happened to the old Bridgette, but I'm sure diggin' the new one."

Bridgette slapped her hand. George tried too, but missed, of course.

***

Later that evening about five blocks away from the Las Vegas strip, a mom and her two children were walking into an ice cream parlor alongside many other stores that lined the busy street.

"Okay, you can both get one scoop, but that's it," said their mom.

"Ah, mom," complained her son, "but I'm 10 now, two years older than Meghan. I should be able to get two scoops."

"One scoop is just fine, mom," said Meghan. She smiled and raised her chin like she was happy and content with her mother's decision.

When he thought his mom wasn't looking, Steve smacked his sister in the back of the head. "How's that for a scoop?"

Their mother saw what he had done from the corner of her eye and shouted, "Steven Simmons! You say you're sorry right this instant!"

Steve lowered his head a bit, ashamed that he had gotten caught. "Uh, sorry, sis." He turned toward his mom to see if that was good enough.

His mom moved up in line, passing the long window of flavored ice cream tubs, and placed her order. "One chocolate cone with *two* scoops, please."

Steve's mouth dropped open.

The attendant handed her the cone. She paid for it and then turned to Meghan. "Here you go, dear. You can have Steve's scoop also."

Steve glared at Meghan, who was happy as could be. Her eyes grew wide as she brought the cone toward her mouth. She gave Steve an arrogant smirk. She smiled and stuck out her tongue to get that first lick right in front of her bratty older brother.

Suddenly, a bell rang, and the front door to the store flew open and smacked Meghan's arm, the one holding that scrumptious treat. The top scoop tumbled to the floor before Meghan's tongue had a chance to taste it. Meghan and Steve traded facial expressions. Her smile turned to a frown, and Steve couldn't help but grin with satisfaction.

The door had been thrust open by a woman with long, dark, messy hair. Her clothes were wrinkled and torn, and she reeked of urine. Meghan gazed up into her bloodshot eyes and trembled. The woman stared at the ice cream cone for a brief moment before snatching it from Meghan's hand. Meghan shrieked and started crying. Steve started snickering while their mother grabbed her distraught daughter's arm and pulled her away from the disgusting woman.

Instead of trying to savor it like a normal person, the woman stuffed the ice cream cone in her mouth and started chewing as if she didn't even have a tongue to taste with. It was gone in four bites. The woman licked the ice cream from her fingers and looked through the glass window at all the tubs of ice cream. Wasting no time at all, she ran around the counter and started digging with her dirty fingernails into the first tub of ice cream she came across. She scooped with four fingers and brought the chocolate ice cream to her mouth, smearing it all over face as she tried her best to stuff it between her lips. Repeatedly, she did this while the young, female store clerk and the family of three watched in horror, speechless.

Moments later the bell rang again, and the glass door smashed open. Two security guards stormed into the establishment. The first one to enter said, "Everyone remain calm. Slowly, with no sudden movements, I want you to exit the building."

The crazed woman kept eating, seemingly unaware of the security guards' presence. The family of three and the high school girl who would probably soon quit her job scooping ice cream, slowly stepped out of the parlor.

The second security guard withdrew his taser from its holster and said, "I got this." He raised his gun and shot the woman in the chest. Instantly she dropped to the floor and lay there fidgeting.

Only minutes after the family had left the building, they sat in their car and watched the security guards haul the woman out of the parlor, one holding her arms while the other grabbed her legs. They carried her to a black SUV, handcuffed her arms behind her, placed her in the back, and then sped out of the parking lot.

Chapter 12

The bell rang, and all eight students grabbed their pencils from Ms. Leadbetter's podium and sat down at their desks. Ms. Leadbetter, dressed in an olive green business suit, wrote the time on the whiteboard and began walking around the room.

George waited for her to pass his desk before he tried to move his pencil. He had to stare at it pretty hard, but he managed to move it a couple of inches.

"I did it!" yelled George. "It moved!"

Immediately, Ms. leadbetter spun around and walked swiftly to his desk. "Do it again," she commanded.

He stared at it, and it rolled an inch this time.

"It's not a strong push, but it did move," observed Ms. Leadbetter. She walked up to the board and wrote down the time and put George's name next to it.

Before she could even finish spelling George's name, Bridgette yelled out, "I did it too!"

Ms. Leadbetter turned and stared at Bridgette while finishing her writing on the board without looking at it.

"Again!" crowed Ms. Leadbetter.

Bridgette barely had to try, and the pencil flew off her desk.

"Excellent!" Ms. Leadbetter wrote down the time again, one minute past George's time, and put Bridgette's name next to it. "You both took longer than me, but that may not mean anything at all. There are so many variables in this project, we can't know how much *time* really affects the strength of your ability."

Bridgette bent down and picked up her pencil, hoping she hadn't moved it so forcefully that Ms. Leadbetter would suspect her of hitting her with it on the first day. And then she realized that she wasn't just hoping that; she was thinking it loudly in her mind. She froze and glanced upward at her instructor.

Ms. Leadbetter was staring at her, kind of like she was trying to figure something out. "I'm sorry, Bridgette; did you say something?"

Bridgette had to think fast. "I was just thinking that my pencil flew off my desk almost as far as George's pencil flew on the first day when he threw it at you."

Ms. Leadbetter shook her head a couple of times, as if she were erasing the thought from her mind.

Quickly, Bridgette started feeding thoughts to her, thoughts like *I can't believe I'm finally able to move my pencil. This stuff really works. I can't wait to tell my parents.*

"Well," said Ms. Leadbetter, "I didn't come prepared today for anyone to move their pencil so you two can go to lunch early. We'll move forward with your training tomorrow."

She didn't have to tell them twice. George and Bridgette grabbed their backpacks and walked toward the door. Bridgette glanced at Janice.

Don't go to lunch without me, thought Janice.

Bridgette heard it in her mind. At first she didn't realize it. She thought Janice had actually spoken it aloud. She nodded at her like she understood.

You heard that? thought Janice.

Bridgette's eyes grew big. She nodded again.

George opened the door, and he and Bridgette walked out of the classroom.

Once on the other side of the door, Bridgette said, "Follow me."

Where are we going? thought George, speed-walking while trying to catch up to her.

"You'll see."

"Hey!" exclaimed George. "Did you just read my-"

"Yes, now be quiet before Ms. Leadbetter finds out."

Bridgette led them down the hall and to the right at the next intersection. She kept reading the signs on the doors to see which rooms they were passing: ENGLISH, HISTORY, FINE ARTS.... After about eight doors, she stopped.

"I think this is it," said Bridgette.

"What?" asked George.

"Read the sign."

George looked up at the sign on the door. "It says DREAM WEAVING. Hey, do you think-"

"Bingo," said Bridgette. She was looking through the rectangular glass on the door. "There they are."

"Let me see," urged George. Bridgette stepped aside and allowed him to peek. Wicked Wanda, Cathy, Maria, and a few of the other girls they had encountered in the cafeteria were sitting in class with their eyes closed. They looked like they were sleeping while at their desks.

"No," said Bridgette.

"No?" repeated George. "No what?"

"No, I can't read their minds to see what they're thinking about."

"This mind-reading is gonna take some getting used to," sighed George.

"Come on," said Bridgette. She started walking back down the hallway. "Stop thinking about lunch. Let's go back to class and wait for Janice. She's expecting us to wait for her."

After a few minutes of waiting outside the door, the bell rang, and Ms. Leadbetter's other six students strolled out of the room.

When Janice walked out, George said, "Anybody else?"

"Nope, you were the only two today," replied Janice. She took the sling off her neck and let her arm, dangle at her side.

"What are you doing?" asked Bridgette.

"I'm not going to give them the satisfaction," answered Janice. "We can't let them think that they got to us. We need to fix this today, or they're just gonna keep haunting us in our dreams."

Are you ready to use your powers to take on Wanda? thought Janice to Bridgette.

"If I have to," said Bridgette.

"Hey," complained George. "Are you reading Janice's mind? No fair. No reading minds until I can do it too."

"How strong is your ability, George?" asked Janice.

"Wait a minute," said George. "Are we at least going to eat lunch first? I'm hungry."

"Come on, Whiz," said Janice. "We've gotta take the fight straight to them. No more letting them tell us where we can and can't eat. This time, we take *their* table. I know you like to be first at everything. Just don't be the first one to run."

"She's right, George," said Bridgette. "They control what happens in our dreams, but we can control what happens when we're awake. If they fear us, they'll respect us and leave us alone."

"Then it's agreed," said Janice. "Follow my lead, and don't look scared. Remember, we have the power when we're awake." She glanced at Bridgette.

Sheepishly, George said, "So Bridgette and I will stand back so we can concentrate and fight with our minds."

Janice put her hand on George's shoulder. "Bring your pencil, Wizard. You might be able to amaze them with it."

George's smile disappeared. "Hey, my power's growing," he said in a high-pitched voice. "And it's Whiz, not Wizard."

"Just make sure you protect Bridgette. She's our secret weapon."

"Wow," said Bridgette. "I've never been called a weapon before. It sounds dangerous."

"Well, don't let it go to your head quite yet," responded Janice. "It's more like you're our *mysterious* weapon because we don't really know how powerful you are yet."

"I hope I don't hurt anyone," admitted Bridgette.

"I hope you do," replied Janice, "and I hope it's Wanda."

By the time they reached the cafeteria, Wanda and her girls had already paid for their diet sodas and were walking away from the cash registers with the cans sitting on top of their trays.

Janice lengthened her stride. "Quick, before they find a table."

They followed close behind, and just as Wanda was about to claim a table for her girls, Janice ran right in front of her and plopped down in one of the chairs. She looked up at Wanda with a smirk. "Looks like you *maggots* are gonna have to find another table."

Wanda's mouth widened in shock, and then she glared down at Janice. "Did you not learn your lesson last night?"

"Last night?" said Janice, pretending to not know what she was talking about.

Wanda grabbed Janice's hurt arm unsuspectingly and said, "Yeah, *you* remember."

Janice winced in pain while she jerked her arm away from Wanda's clutches.

That was all Janice needed to spark the anger that burned deep within her. She grasped onto Wanda's arm, and, like making a chalkboard screech with sharp fingernails, she dug deeply into Wanda's skin and clawed all the way down her arm, creating instant streaks of blood. And just *like* a chalkboard, Wanda screeched as well, only much louder and with a higher pitch.

Maria and Cathy moved in to rescue their friend. That's when George and Bridgette began their own attack. Bridgette focused on Maria because she looked the fiercer of the two. With pure concentration, she stared intensely on her legs. Just before Maria reached Janice, she began to rise in the air.

"What the..." blurted out Maria.

Maria and Cathy both turned toward Bridgette and understood what was happening. Cathy changed directions and started toward Bridgette to interrupt her focus.

"I got her," said George. He glared at Cathy and instantly her hair began to rise slowly in the air. When he realized his power was far too weak to stop her, he gulped.

Bridgette must have been anticipating George's weakness. She held out her hand like a police officer trying to get someone to stop his car. Simultaneously, Cathy's legs locked up, and she almost fell forward on her face, but she didn't. Instead, she wobbled, trying as best as she could to not fall over.

"Let me go!" screamed Cathy.

While still holding onto Wanda's bloody arm, Janice turned around and smiled. She yanked on Wanda's body, one hand around the back of her neck and the other on her arm, and led her toward Maria. She twisted Wanda's arm and clobbered Maria across the nose with it. Blood smeared all over Maria's face.

"Ahhhh!" yelled Maria in disgust. She smeared the blood across her cheeks even more with her own hands while trying to wipe it off. She couldn't clear it completely from her face, however, because her nose was doing some bleeding of its own.

A crowd of students began to form a circle around the altercation.

Next, Janice forced Wanda to stumble toward Cathy.

"No!" hollered Cathy.

This time Janice used Wanda's bloody arm to swipe upward at Cathy's nose. Upon impact, Cathy rose a couple of inches off the ground before falling on her butt. Instinctively, she reached for her broken nose and smeared a mixture of Wanda's and her own blood all over her face.

Instantly, whistles were blowing and three security officers were scrambling toward the fight. They were carrying black clubs in one hand in case they needed to use them.

The officer in charge, an unshaven Caucasian man, wearing a blue uniform and black cap, spit out his whistle that was tied to a string around his neck. He pushed a few spectators aside and said, "What seems to be the problem, ladies?"

Janice spoke first. "No problem here that we can't fix ourselves, officer."

With her freckled hands cupping her nose, Cathy cried, "She broke my nose." Blood bubbled through her fingers while she tried to speak.

The officer looked at Janice. "Is this true?"

"Well, I don't know if it's broken," admitted Janice with a smirk, "but I think I did hear a *pop* when her friend's arm slammed up against it."

He glanced over at Wanda's bloody arm. "You hit this girl? That her blood on your arm?"

"Oh, please!" hollered Wanda. "Come on, officer, use some detective skills for crying out loud. Look at the scratches on my arm, and then look at the bloody fingernails of this Neanderthal chick." She nodded at Janice.

"All right, that's it. All y'all come with us. We're gonna get some names and then we're gonna find out who your teachers are, and if they discover that you used your special abilities here today to do harm to one another, then y'all gonna be in a big world of hurt."

Janice looked at Bridgette and thought, *Do you wanna make a run for it?*

Bridgette shook her head.

All six girls were marched out of the cafeteria. Janice was at the end of the line with an officer's club poking her in the back.

Back at the security office, the Dream Weavers' teacher showed up first. He was wearing glasses and was dressed in a white lab coat. "Sorry, officer, I came as quickly as I could."

"Officer Halfpenny," he replied with an outstretched hand.

"Officer Halfpenny," repeated the teacher while shaking his hand. "I'm Mr. Pleasant. You must be new here. You don't look familiar."

"Been here couple months now," replied Officer Halfpenny. He removed his cap, exposing his red hair. "I may be somewhat new, but I know shenanigans when I see 'em. Now, I heard these here kids are all working on some special abilities so if you tell me what I should be looking for, I might be able to let you know if they was using 'em."

"Was everybody awake?" asked Mr. Pleasant.

"Everybody I saw," answered Mr. Halfpenny.

"Then they weren't using any special abilities, at least not any of *my* students."

"Well, what about *these* here kids?" asked the security officer, motioning with his hand at Janice, Bridgette, and George.

"You'll have to talk to *their* teacher. May I take my students now?"

"Well, sure, but don't they wanna file a report about they faces? One's got a broken nose fo' sho'."

"We're okay," said Cathy. "We just want to go home now."

Wanda gazed down at the blood-soaked bandage on her arm and snarled.

Officer Halfpenny said to her, "You look like you wanna kill somebody."

Wanda wiped the look off her face. "Oh, my arm just hurts. That's all."

"Change that bandage I gave you when you get home."

She smiled, but it looked more like a grimace. Walking past Bridgette, she raised a hand and opened and closed it like she was talking with her fingers. "Ta ta, maggots."

Mr. Pleasant led them out of the room and down the hall back toward his classroom.

Obviously agitated, Bridgette's mind began to fog up. All the noise in the room disappeared as if she were standing alone. A vision began to form in her mind. She witnessed an image of Mr. Pleasant walking down the hall with his students. When they walked inside his classroom, Mr. Pleasant struck Wanda across the face with the back of his hand and said, "I thought I told you three to stay out of trouble." He was wearing a ring, and it left a red welt on her right cheek.

A knock at the door broke Bridgette from her trance. It was Ms. Leadbetter.

Officer Halfpenny opened the door. "You must be Ms. Leadbetter."

"And you must be…..don't tell me…….Mr. Halfpenny."

Even Bridgette could hear him thinking *Mr. Halfpenny* in her mind.

"How did you know? This is just my second day. Is that a special ability y'all teaching these girls?"

Ms. Leadbetter replied, "It is. It's called being observant." She pointed at his shirt.

He looked down. "Oh, my name badge." He chuckled. "You *had* me there for a minute."

She did the same thing to me, thought Bridgette, remembering back to her first day of class.

Ms. Leadbetter glanced at Bridgette after her thought escaped.

Oops.

"I'll take care of things from here, officer. Thank you for contacting me."

Officer Halfpenny pinched the bill of his cap. "My pleasure, ma'am. Any peculiar things I should be keeping a lookout for?"

Ms. Leadbetter smiled. "Nothing to concern yourself with, officer. Their special abilities will take years to develop."

"Just trying to stay ahead of the game is all."

Ms. Leadbetter's eyes twinkled. "Oh, but the game hasn't even started yet."

They all walked into the long hallway.

"Y'all stay out of trouble now," said Officer Halfpenny.

"Oh, but it's so hard to stay out of trouble," said Ms. Leadbetter, "when you're already *in* trouble. Right children?"

Bridgette looked far down the hallway and saw someone walking toward them. Then she received another vision, just like the one a few minutes ago. Ms. Leadbetter had George closed in her classroom alone. She seemed to be interrogating him. "So, George, tell me, have any of you been using your abilities outside of the classroom?"

George stood there, motionless. Speechless.

"I see. And what have you done?"

"What? I didn't say anything," said George nervously.

"You didn't have to."

Bridgette bumped into the wall while walking and broke from her vision.

"Bridgette," said George. "Answer Ms. Leadbetter. Do you want to come with us to talk more about our special ability?"

Bridgette looked at Janice. She read her mind. She was going home.

"No, I've got to get home early today. Perhaps tomorrow."

"Suit yourself," replied George.

Just then Wanda passed them in the hallway. She had a big red mark on her cheek. Bridgette's jaw dropped as if she had just discovered something important because she had.

"Stare much?" spat Wanda with a snotty tone.

"Uh, George," called Bridgette.

He and Ms. Leadbetter, who had both been walking away from them, turned around.

"Aren't you forgetting something?"

"Huh?" George looked confused.

"You're supposed to help me make that surprise for that special someone. Your parents will get upset if you don't."

"Go ahead, George," said Ms. Leadbetter, "we can all have a chat tomorrow during class."

Bridgette held out her arm and motioned for George to walk toward him. "Come on. Let's hurry before we're late."

"Well, okay," agreed George. "See you tomorrow, Ms. Leadbetter."

They walked outside into the gusty wind, leaving Ms. Leadbetter alone to stare after them.

Once the door shut, George starting thinking in his head: *Why can't I stay with Ms. Leadbetter? This would be … …*

Bridgette heard it all in her mind until a strong gust of wind blew past them. It's as if the wind carried away his thoughts.

"This would be what?" asked Bridgette.

"This would be the perfect chance for me to find out what Ms. Leadbetter has in store for us next."

"You guys wanna clue me in on the conversation," said Janice.

"Let's go back to my house," said Bridgette, "and I'll tell you everything."

During their fifteen minute walk home, Bridgette couldn't stop thinking that not only could she get glimpses of the future, but she thought she could alter them as well since it seemed like she just prevented Ms. Leadbetter from cornering George in the classroom.

Chapter 13

After Bridgette had explained what was going on to the others back at her place in the confines her bedroom, she said, "So you see, we can't be alone with Ms. Leadbetter, or she'll try to get us to snitch on each other."

They were all sitting on Bridgette's bed, which had a pink blanket with colorful unicorns prancing on it. Their backs were against the wall while their shoes dangled off the short edge.

"We're not gonna tell," admitted Janice.

"Of course we're not," agreed Bridgette, "at least not with our mouths. But if she can read our minds like I can read yours, and I think she can, then we can't be trusted with what our minds might say. If I've learned one thing from church, it's that we're all sinners, no matter how hard we try to be good. We can ask God for forgiveness, and Ms. Leadbetter is *not* God, no matter how high and mighty she might think she is."

"Yes," agreed George, "and the moment she finds out, we're all toast."

They looked at Janice to concur.

Janice snarled, "Forgiveness is for chumps. You got one part right though, the part about us being sinners. I'm an original sinner."

"What does that even *mean?*" asked Bridgette.

Janice almost chuckled but then coughed instead. "I don't know. I heard it in a song once, and I thought it was cool."

"Okay, then it's agreed," said Bridgette. "Don't let Ms. Leadbetter get any of us alone.

"Now that that's settled, let's talk more about my visions of the future."

George rubbed his chin like he was thinking hard. "We've got to be able to use this to our advantage, and knowing that we can actually see the future and then change it before it happens is huge."

"But I can't control it," whined Bridgette. "I don't know what turns it on and off."

"Can you remember what you were thinking of both times it happened?" asked George.

"Well," replied Bridgette, "the first time was right after Wanda and her bunch were walking away from us outside the security office."

"And the second time?" urged George.

"The second time," repeated Bridgette, almost as a reflex while she thought about it. "The second time is when Ms. Leadbetter was telling us something about not being able to stay out of trouble or something. She was trying to be witty, I think. Ugh, I try to like everybody I come across, but I can't find anything redeemable about that woman."

"So what's the connection?" asked Janice. "There's Wanda the first time and Ms. Leadbottom the second."

"That's it!" exclaimed George.

"What?" asked Bridgette.

"You hate both of them," pronounced George as if he had just solved a murder mystery.

Bridgette thought for a moment. "Well, hate is such a strong word. I'm not sure I really *hate* anyone. I think Wanda is just a bit misguided though."

"What?" said George and Janice at the same time.

"Everyone deserves second chances," replied Bridgette.

Bridgette could hear both of them thinking about Ms. Leadbetter's second chance.

"And Ms. Leadbetter has had plenty of second chances," she said aloud so that they could both hear her answer.

"Maybe there doesn't *have* to be a connection," suggested Janice.

"Wait!" shouted Bridgette. "As I recall, I was angry with Wanda because she was snarling like she wanted to kill someone, like what Officer Halfpenny said. And Ms. Leadebetter was trying to be witty with her smart remark about staying *out* of trouble while being *in* trouble."

"So that's it then," pronounced George. "The trigger is anger."

Bridgette nodded. "Must be."

Janice scooted closer to Bridgette on the bed. "Let's try it out."

"I'm not an angry person by nature," admitted Bridgette.

"That's stating the obvious," said Janice smartly. She shoved Bridgette in the shoulder. "We just need to *make* you angry."

"Hey, you can't toy with my emotions like that."

George shoved her in the other shoulder. "But how else are we gonna make you mad?"

"Well, *that's* not going to work," declared Bridgette.

"Then what?" asked Janice.

Bridgette thought for a moment. "I don't know. Maybe an injustice in the world or something."

"A what?" asked Janice.

"An injustice," said George, jumping in. "You know, something that someone does that's wrong, and he gets away with it."

"Oh, you mean like throwing a cat off a freeway bridge or something like that," said Janice.

"I suppose that would do it," thought Bridgette aloud. She quickly added, "Don't even think about it."

Janice threw her hands up in the air in disgust. "That's just great. You have the greatest gift, but you can't use it. Why would a gift like this be given to such a nice person who rarely gets mad? I could use this power all day long."

"Why *are* you angry all the time?" asked Bridgette.

"Nice try," said Janice. "The answer to *that* question is not going to solve our problem."

"Ok, well, let's work on something I *do* know how to control," suggested Bridgette. She scooted off her bed, took three steps away, and then stared at it. Slowly, the bed began to rise off the ground while still holding George and Janice.

George clung onto the bedspread as if it would save him from falling off.

"That's impressive," said Janice. "You're able to move a lot more weight than what good ole Leadbottom thinks."

"Remember," added George, "she shouldn't lift more than me, or Ms. Leadbetter might think something's up. I have to be first in everything. It's the natural way."

"I don't think there's anything natural about it," responded Janice. "I just wonder if and when I'm ever going to do it."

Just then there was a loud knock on the door. "Bridgette, honey," said her mom through the door, "I've got a plate of cookies for you guys. May I come in?"

Bridgette lost her focus, and the bed plopped about two feet to the floor.

Bridgette's mom decided not to wait for an answer. After hearing the loud thud, she hastily pushed the door open. "What was that?"

"Sorry, Mom," said Bridgette. "I was lifting the bed with my mind, and you startled me."

Bridgette's mom handed the plate of cookies to her. "I hope you're not showing off."

"Mom, you know me better than that."

Her mother pointed at her. "Remember, daughter of mine, you're only 12. You still have a lot to learn."

"That's why I'm practicing."

"I was talking about life, not your new ability," responded her mom.

"I was just testing my strength. It's getting easier, and I can move heavier objects."

"Ok, well don't lift anything heavy in the house; you might break something." She walked out the room and closed the door behind her.

"Does your mom know you can read minds or see into the future?" asked George.

"No," replied Bridgette, "and I want to keep it that way. If she ever talks to Ms. Leadbetter, she'd be able to read her mind and find out. We need to make sure nobody else knows."

"Look," cried George, "I'm getting stronger too." He stared at the bed, and with much labor and concentration, the edge of the blanket slowly lifted in the air. As if he had been holding his breath the entire time, he blew out a burst of air, and the blanket relaxed once again.

"Nice job, George," said Bridgette.

"Yeah," replied Janice, "I'll let you know if I need someone to save me from making my own bed."

"I'll catch up," said George. "And what about you? *You* haven't even moved your pencil yet."

"Hmph, I don't need my mind to move things," scoffed Janice. "I've got these." She held up her hands and bunched them into fists.

"Those'll make *me* move all right," declared George.

"Ok, I'll see you at school tomorrow, Janice," said Bridgette.

Janice looked at her funny.

Bridgette put her hand up to her mouth. "I'm so sorry. That must have sounded pretty bad, huh? I'm not asking you to leave. I heard your thoughts in my head, and I wasn't even trying. You *were* thinking you had to get home, right?"

Janice nodded. "Your powers are growing fast, and you don't even practice."

"Remember," said Bridgette with a hint of warning, "we can't let Ms. Leadbetter find out how strong I'm getting. I'm just going to progress at the speed of George, no more than that."

"Wait," said George, "aren't we gonna talk about Wanda before we split up? What if she comes after us in our sleep again?"

"If she does," answered Janice, "there's nothing we can do about it tonight."

"All right, I'm gonna go home too," said George.

"I knew you were gonna say that," said Bridgette smiling.

"I'm glad you're on our side," said George. Then he looked at Janice. "And I'm glad you are too."

Chapter 14

George and Janice walked outside into the darkness together. The full moon hovered above them, keeping watch on everything it could see. The soft whistling wind whirled past them.

"You want me to walk you home?" asked George, trying to be a gentleman.

"Nah, I can take care of myself," replied Janice. "I doubt anyone will need their bed to be made while I'm walking home tonight, and mine's already been made." She chuckled.

George looked down at the ground, obviously insulted by the remark. "I'm gonna practice all night tonight. You'll see; my powers are going to get stronger."

"We all gotta start somewhere, Whiz." She patted her hand on his shoulder in a consoling manner as she walked toward the darkened street.

George lifted his head. "Be careful."

Without turning around, Janice responded, "Always."

Janice lived about a twenty-minute walk away if she took the streets, fifteen minutes if she cut through the alleys. It was getting late so she decided to take as many shortcuts as she could.

The first alley was small and lit fairly well by a tall streetlight. A dog barked at her from behind a fence. It startled her, only because she was a bit nervous being alone at night at such a late hour.

Her heartbeat began to slow while she turned back toward the street to follow the sidewalk for a ways.

Minutes later she came to another alley, one that would easily shave three minutes off her time. There were no streetlights in the area, so it was considerably darker than the last shortcut. She stopped and stared, trying to pierce the darkness with her vision but unable to. She suspected it was easily one, possibly two, blocks deep because she couldn't see any lights or cars at the other end. In fact, she couldn't see the other end because of the blackness that concealed everything within it.

Janice turned her ear toward the alleyway and listened. Nothing. She whispered, "One, two, three," and then began walking into the dark unknown. She walked slowly since she could barely see. It was a narrow passageway barely enough room for a car to drive through. It appeared to be walled off by fences or the backs of houses; it was too difficult to tell.

After about 25 steps she kicked a small rock, at least she thought it was *her* that kicked it. She stopped and listened. Her heart was thumping hard, so hard she thought she might even hear it if she listened close enough. Silence. In a small panic, she picked up the pace.

Thirty seconds later she noticed a light flickering ahead. *Finally*, she thought. *I thought this alley would never end.*

She walked even faster. That's when she heard a pebble skittering across the ground again, and this time she *knew* it wasn't from her because it came from far behind.

Janice wasn't normally one to scare so easily, but fear of the unknown is a lot to ask of *anyone* to overcome. Her walk became a trot. The more she ran, the more scared she became until she found herself running as fast as she could as if her life depended on it.

The flickering light was getting closer and closer. While she closed in on it, she realized it was a fire, a fire inside a barrel. People were huddled around it for warmth. She couldn't see their faces, but she could tell their clothing was tattered and torn.

Bums, she thought. *Well, at least I'm safe from whoever was following me.*

Janice stopped running and walked cautiously toward the burning barrel. She turned around, but it was too dark to see anything. She walked up to the people with their hands held up to the barrel, almost like they were worshipping it in a circle.

"You guys staying warm?" asked Janice with nothing better to say.

All heads jerked in her direction. Their eyes bulged white with jagged red veins running like crooked rivers throughout. At once, they lunged at her. One hand wrapped around her arm, but she yanked it free. Hurriedly, she tried to continue running the way she thought was toward her house. After only a couple of steps, she realized it was a dead end. There were too many bodies in front of her. She would have to go back the same way she had entered. She backed up a few steps and then turned and ran right into the chest of a tall teenaged boy, almost an adult, who stared into her eyes from far above her head. He wrapped his arms around her tightly. There must have been a scream being held prisoner deep within Janice's lungs for many years because when it was finally squeezed out of her, it rattled the neighborhood.

After the desperate scream's echo faded, Janice heard a familiar voice coming from the other side of the alley, the way she had entered. "Over here, Janice! This Way!"

Janice ducked and slid out of the young man's arms, escaping his grasp. She ran toward the voice in the darkness. The fiery barrel was blazing on her right with people running toward her. Barely recognizing George's face, she sprinted toward him.

When George saw her coming, he turned and started running like a madman.

Janice could hear footsteps charging from behind. "George, we're not gonna make it!"

"Just keep running!" George stopped at the entrance of the alley toward the corner where Janice shot past. He dropped in the darkness to his hands and knees, closed his eyes, and waited for the impact.

Sure enough the tall teen collided with George and flew right over him, tumbling on the pavement. He let out a few moans.

Stunned, the teen tried to shake the cobwebs from his head and stand. That gave George enough time to pick himself up and chase after Janice.

Janice had made it almost all the way home before George caught up to her. He was holding onto his ribs with his right hand.

"Are you okay?" asked Janice.

"Yeah, got kicked in the ribs when I tripped that guy chasing you."

Janice gave a look of admiration to George and said, "Guts, man. You've got guts. Have I ever told you that?"

"Once or twice," replied George. He laughed and then winced while holding onto his ribs again.

"This still doesn't mean you need to walk me home. It just means I need to stay on a lit path."

George shook his head. "It means you shouldn't be walking home in the dark. Period."

"That'll work too," agreed Janice.

Chapter 15

Later that night shortly after Bridgette went to bed, she heard tapping sounds on her bedroom window. Wearing a long orange t-shirt that went down to her knees, she crawled out of bed. She peeled back the curtains and then jumped back with a startle. Wanda's face was so close to her window, her nose was almost pressed up against it.

I wonder if this is another dream, thought Bridgette.

Bridgette slid the window open. "What are you doing here?"

"We need to have a talk," replied Wanda. "Come on out here; I don't want to pull your parents into this dream."

"You're in my dream again?" asked Bridgette.

"No, you're in mine."

"Prove it," challenged Bridgette, not totally sure if she was dreaming or not.

Bridgette's porch light lit up the yard enough for her to watch the show.

Wanda lifted her arms up by her sides and rose from the ground about five feet. She gave Bridgette a look that seemed to say, "Satisfied?"

Apparently, she was because Bridgette climbed through the opening in the window and plopped to the ground outside. She looked left and then right. "Where's your backup?"

"I don't need backup in my dream world," snarled Wanda. "Nothing happens in here unless I want it to."

"How did they teach you how to do this?" asked Bridgette, hoping to find out her secret.

"You think I'd tell you?" asked Wanda rhetorically.

Bridgette stared intensely at Wanda, trying to read her mind to gain the secret of dream weaving, but it was no use. It was like trying to read the mind of a rock.

Wanda assumed Bridgette was trying to use her powers. "As I said before, your abilities won't work here. This is *my* dream and *your* nightmare." She flew toward Bridgette and wrapped her arm around her, putting her in a choke hold.

Remembering the last time she was in one of Wanda's dreams, Bridgette didn't panic. She waited to see if she would feel pain or loss of breath. She didn't.

Wanda cranked and cranked on her choke hold, smiling while thinking she was really squeezing the life out of Bridgette until finally Bridgette said in a normal voice, "Are you done yet? I'd really like to get back to my own dreams."

"That's impossible!" cried Wanda. "I thought it was a fluke last time." She unleashed her arm from around Bridgette's neck.

"I'm afraid not," said Bridgette. "I guess my mind knows this is just a dream, and because I realize that, I know I can't be hurt."

"Then how do you explain the others?"

Bridgette thought for a moment. "Perhaps their minds aren't convinced it's a dream."

"But you were screaming the last time," Wanda reminded Bridgette. "That means you didn't know it was a dream at the time."

Bridgette didn't have an answer for that one. It's true. She hadn't realized it was a dream until after she had woken up.

"Anyway, are we done here?" asked Bridgette. "I'd like to get back to my regular sleep."

"Nope, I guess I'm just going to have to haunt you in your dreams until you agree to help me."

"Help you?" asked Bridgette. "That's what this is all about? You want my help?"

"Well, yeah, and you better or else I'm not going anywhere," commanded Wanda.

"Why didn't you just ask me for help instead of try to force me to?"

"Would you have?"

Bridgette thought about it. "It all depends on what you need help with, I guess. Why don't you tell me what it is so I can decide?"

"Well," began Wanda, "we thought if we could get the help of the Aces, we-"

"Aces?" said Bridgette.

"Yeah, Aces. That's what we call you brainiacs in the Mind over Matter class. "As I was saying…""

"Sorry," said Bridgette.

Wanda continued, "There's a group of kids about a half-mile from here. We call them Berserkers."

"Berserkers?"

"Did I stutter?" said Wanda smartly. "They live in the shadows between the buildings like homeless people. The cops don't dare go there. The Berserkers don't follow any rules, and they don't respect authority or anybody for that matter. They like to hunt in packs."

"Did you say hunt?" asked Bridgette.

"That's what I said. They're barbarians. They take what they want and need. They're brainless. It's like they can't think of anything except for food and shelter."

"So why tell *me* about them?"

"They've got my little sister."

"Are you sure?"

"Their leader - he doesn't really talk - we call him the Alpha. I brought him into one of my dreams. I tortured him, but it was no use. He either can't or won't speak."

"So then how do you know he took your sister?"

"I know because he held up Sissy's doll and laughed at me," replied Wanda.

"This really sounds like a job for the police," said Bridgette.

"I already told you the police won't step foot in that part of town. If you won't do it to help save my sister, do it to save some of your class members."

"What?" asked Bridgette.

"It's ironic that they call you Aces when you're the last ones to find out. All the Aces in the class that don't develop special abilities begin to slowly transform into Berserkers. Remember that shot they gave you on your first day?"

Bridgette nodded.

"We got it too. The same thing happens to us Dream Weavers. It all starts with a mild headache, and then the headaches start to get worse and worse, eventually killing your brain. All that's left is the will to survive at any and all costs. Eventually, you find yourself sleeping in the alley, hanging out with all the homeless people."

Bridgette's thoughts immediately jumped to Janice. She hadn't gained any abilities yet.

"How long does it take to start getting the headaches after you've received the shot?" asked Bridgette.

"No one knows. I guess it all depends on the person. Why? Do you know someone who hasn't gained any abilities yet?"

Bridgette nodded. "Not everyone in my class has gotten them, at least not yet."

"So, will you help me?" asked Wanda.

"I'll do it on two conditions," said Bridgette. "One: you have to stop picking on my friends and me."

"And two?" said Wanda with her arms crossed.

Bridgette smiled. "It seems like such a waste to only have three people sit at those big cafeteria tables. I'd like us to start eating together, at the same table."

Wanda closed her eyes as if it pained her to hear such a request. When she opened them, they were glossy. "Do you mean that after all my friends and I have put you through, you actually *want* us to eat with you? Who *are* you?"

"I'm the girl who's going to help you get your sister back," said Bridgette. "So, is it a deal?" Bridgette held out her hand.

Reluctantly, Wanda said, "It's a deal, but I'm not touching your hand."

Bridgette lifted her hand higher. "How about hitting it?"

"That would still be touching, duh."

Bridgette stared at Wanda and smiled. "You may act tough, but there's a nice and caring person trapped somewhere deep inside you. I can even hear her sometimes."

"Oh yeah," sneered Wanda. "And what is she saying?"

Bridgette was hoping for that question. "She's saying, 'Help me get my sister.'"

Wanda wiped the sneer from her face. "Let's talk more at lunch tomorrow."

Bridgette lifted her hand and waved. "See you then."

Instantly, she woke from the dream and sat up in her bed. *Did Wanda release me from her dream, or did I leave it on my own?* she wondered.

Before she could come up with an answer, she had already lain back down and had fallen fast asleep.

Chapter 16

The next morning George and Janice showed up early at Bridgette's house. It was unusual as they normally didn't all get together before school.

Bridgette opened the door, and a gust of wind blew her hair back. She squinted her eyes, partially because of the wind but also because of the brightness of the day.

"We've got news," blurted Janice in her jeans jacket. George was standing next to her.

Bridgette beckoned with her hand and smiled. "Come in, I've got news for you two also."

George patted his hair down and closed the door behind them, which caused an even stronger gust of wind to blow some papers off the hallway table.

"Don't worry about it," said Bridgette. "That always happens."

Janice looked around. "Where are your parents?"

"We're in here!" yelled Bridgette's mom from the dining room. "Are you guys hungry?"

"No thanks, uh, Bridgette's mom," said Janice. She looked at Bridgette. "What's your last name?"

"It's Swanson," whispered Bridgette with a smile.

"I mean Mrs. Swanson," Janice corrected herself.

"Of course, I already knew that," said George with a smug look on his face.

"Yes," said Janice, "you probably knew it before they even moved here, right?"

"It's a curse," said George, "always knowing things. If only I could learn to forget."

Janice slugged him in the shoulder. "Well, I'm sure you won't forget that I can still whip you until your powers get a lot stronger."

"Speaking of that," said George. He put his finger to his mouth and motioned for the three of them to go into Bridgette's bedroom for privacy.

"We'll be in my room!" hollered Bridgette to her parents.

Bridgette closed the door behind her. "George, did you practice again last night?"

"I said I would, and I did. Go ahead you two, have a seat on the bed."

Bridgette and Janice sat down. George stared intensely at the bed, and it started to shake.

"Wait," whispered Bridgette. "Remember what happened last time? My mom doesn't want me lifting things in here."

George blew out a deep breath which caused his blonde bangs to lift in the air. "Fine, let's try this instead. Bridgette, stand up."

He obviously chose Bridgette, being the lighter of the two girls.

Bridgette willingly rose and stood on the wooden floor in jeans and polka dotted pink and white socks. She gazed at George with a "you-can-do-it" look.

George stared at her feet. One foot rose from the floor.

"Hey, this feels weird," said Bridgette while wiggling her leg in the air.

Next her other leg floated upward. She was floating toward the ceiling.

"You did it, George!" exclaimed Bridgette.

George's face was as red as a ripe tomato, and then it started turning blue.

Bridgette's mouth dropped. "George, breathe," she ordered. She raised her palms and pressed them against the ceiling.

George let out a gigantic breath, releasing his hold on Bridgette. She squealed while falling to the floor, but she caught herself with her own powers before landing. She held her arms outward with her palms upward like she had seen Wanda do in the dream last night, only she was suspending herself in the air for real, not just in a dream.

"That's just creepy," said Janice.

Bridgette allowed herself to fall slowly and stand on her own.

"Sorry about that," said George sheepishly.

"I am so impressed, George," said Bridgette. She looked at Janice. "Isn't that great, Janice?"

"Yeah, it's cool. I just wish it would start working for me."

"That reminds me of the news I wanted to tell you about," said Bridgette.

Suddenly, Janice squeezed her eyes shut and groaned. It lasted only a second, and then she was back to her normal mean-looking snarl.

"What's wrong?" asked Bridgette. She rushed toward Janice as if she were going to catch her from falling.

"Oh, nothing, just a little headache. Woke up with it this morning. Probably slept wrong last night or something.

"So what's the news?"

"The news," repeated Bridgette. She changed gears in her mind and thought up a different topic. "Right, the news. *We* have a nickname."

"A nickname," said George. "How come I didn't know about this? Was it just made up or something?"

"Nope, it's been around since before we started our Mind over Matter class. Apparently, we're called Aces. And that's not all; Wanda's gang is called the Dream Weavers."

"Makes sense," said George. "Now we've got some news of our own."

Bridgette wasn't done with what she had to say but wasn't about to interrupt George, so she listened closely.

George's eyes grew big. "Last night we came across some weird looking homeless people. Something was wrong with their eyes, and they actually tried to attack us."

"*Us?*" asked Bridgette.

"I was there," added Janice.

"You two were together … in the dark?"

"It's not what you think," said George. "I followed Janice to make sure she would get home okay."

"As if I need someone to follow me," snarled Janice.

"Well, not all the time," said George, "but...-"

"But what?" said Janice with an agitated tone. "I told you I can take care of myself." She closed her hands into fists, and her knuckles cracked.

Bridgette gave a nervous smile. "Let's calm down. We're all friends here. Let me ask a question. Were you guys in an alley when you were attacked?"

"How did you know?" asked George. "Were you there watching us?"

Bridgette shook her head. "No, but I know who they are. They're called Berserkers."

"Berserkers?" repeated Janice.

"Yep," said Bridgette, "as in *c r a z y*." She said the word crazy with a high pitched voice.

"How do you know this stuff?" asked George, obviously a bit perturbed that Bridgette knew before him.

"This is the news I've been waiting to tell you," said Bridgette.

George and Janice both stared at her. She looked at them as if waiting for a signal.

"Well, go ahead and spill," demanded Janice.

"With pleasure," said Bridgette. "Wanda pulled me into one of her dreams last night."

Janice rudely interrupted her. "Why that -"

"It's okay," said Bridgette. "Hear me out. She wants my help to save her little sister."

George and Janice both shook their heads.

"Let me finish before you say no," said Bridgette. "The Berserkers have her, and I told her I would help get her back, and in exchange she and her gang will stop bullying us."

"And you believed her?" asked Janice

"Could you read her mind to see if she was just tricking you?" asked George.

"No, I didn't because it was *her* dream. I couldn't get anything, but I believe her. She's really not such a bad person, just misguided."

"Well," said George, "I'd say most bad people are 'misguided.' That's *how* they become bad people in the first place."

Bridgette folded her arms together. "I'm not going to give up on her so easily, and neither should you. We all have our issues."

"We all know Janice's issue," said George, "though we don't know the cause of it."

Janice frowned at him.

George turned his head toward Bridgette. "And I can see your issue, Bridgette. You're too trusting. But what issue could *I* possibly have?"

Janice and Bridgette looked at each other, holding back their laughter.

"Let me take a stab," said Janice. "This requires a mean answer, and I don't think you have it in you, Bridge."

Janice stepped up to George. "George, how many friends do you have?"

George looked confused. "Present company included?"

"Sure," agreed Janice.

He pointed at Bridgette and then at her. "Two."

"Exactly," said Janice. "If it weren't for us, you wouldn't even *have* any friends."

"The same could be said for all of us though," pointed out George.

"Precisely," said Janice, "because we *all* have issues."

"Well, I only choose to have two friends," said George. "My time is too valuable to have more than that."

"George, just admit it," said Janice. "You have issues."

George shook his head.

"Can't you see?" said Janice. "It's staring you right in the face: You can't be wrong. You're a know-it-all."

George's eyes watered up. He shook his head back and forth. "No. No. No."

"It's okay, George," said Bridgette with a soothing voice. She placed her hand gently on his back. "Only a true friend would be bold enough to tell you this."

That only caused the tears to start trickling down his cheeks.

George couldn't let them see him cry, so he bolted from the room and out of the house.

"George! Come back!" yelled Bridgette.

"Do you think I overdid it?" asked Janice. "I mean, *I* don't think I did, but do you?"

"No, you didn't," replied Bridgette. "In fact, I read his mind as he was leaving. He was asking himself if he really *was* a know-it-all.

"Speaking of reading minds," said Bridgette, "I couldn't help but hear you wondering about your recent headache. It's been going on for a couple of days now, hasn't it?"

"Stay out of my head!" commanded Janice.

"I'm worried about you," said Bridgette.

Janice groaned. "First George last night and now you today. Do I have the words HELP ME printed on my forehead?"

"I can't help it," said Bridgette. "I treat my friends like family so you're gonna have to learn to deal with it."

"Fine," blurted Janice. "Thank you."

She said it so harshly that it didn't sound the least bit sincere, but for Janice, it was the best she could do.

Bridgette could read the sincerity in Janice's head though and knew she was truly grateful.

Bridgette smiled. "You know, I think you and Wanda have more in common than you know."

"Don't bet on it," replied Janice.

Lost in thought, Bridgette said to herself, "What to do … what to do."

"Huh?" said Janice.

"Oh," said Bridgette, snapping out of her concentration, "I have a theory about your headaches."

"I'm waiting."

With a serious look, Bridgette said, "Have you been practicing at home like George … you know … to make the pencil move?"

"I told you," responded Janice, "I don't need that stuff. I got these." She put her fists up high in the air.

"Of course," agreed Bridgette, "but *those* are not going to stop your headaches."

"And moving a pencil with my mind *will*?" said Janice. "For all I know, that's why I'm getting the headaches in the first place."

Bridgette nodded her head as if she, herself, were getting closer and closer to figuring out what was wrong. "I think I need to introduce you to somebody."

Janice looked dumbfounded. "What?"

"Remember how George said mean people become mean because they have been misguided?"

"Uh, I think he said 'bad' people, not mean."

"Sorry," said Bridgette. "You know what I mean. Anyway, I think this *person* just might save you in more ways than one."

"Huh?" said Janice. "What else do I need to be saved from? Did you get a vision of the future you're not telling me about?"

"Never mind that now. Just start practicing as much as you can. You've got to make that pencil move. If you can't make the pencil move by tomorrow, I'll let you meet him."

"Him? A man or a boy?"

"Just focus on the pencil like your life depended on it," said Bridgette.

"I don't get it. Is *he* gonna kill me if I can't do it?"

"Not even close. If I told you everything, you wouldn't be able to focus. It's better that you stay in the dark for now.

"Come on. Let's get going to school."

Bridgette slipped on her shoes on and grabbed her backpack. "Mom, we're ready for school!"

Chapter 17

When Janice and Bridgette walked into their Mind over Matter classroom, George was already sitting at his desk.

Hurry and start class, Ms. Leadbetter, so I can show you how much stronger I am today, thought George.

Bridgette coughed to try and get George's attention. She couldn't even think about warning him about his dangerous thoughts because she knew Ms. Leadbetter, who was standing behind her podium, would hear her thoughts as well as his.

Her weak attempt went unnoticed so she sat down in George's view. She tried to give him a serious look of caution, but he purposely turned his head so that he couldn't see her. A tear streamed down her cheek. She gazed over at Ms. Leadbetter who was scowling in George's direction.

The bell rang, and the last student entered the room and scurried to her seat. Still staring at George, Ms. Leadbetter paid no attention to the tardy girl.

Finally, Ms. Leadbetter started class. "Okay, class, you have a pencil on your desk. You know what to do. Bridgette and George, I'll meet with you in the back of the room."

Quickly, she wrote the time on the whiteboard before picking up a clipboard and swishing in her black pants to the far end of the room.

"Have a seat," whispered Ms. Leadbetter.

Bridgette and George both sat down at the two desks that were waiting for them.

"Bridgette, we'll start with you. Stare at that desk over there." She was pointing at one of the many empty desks, one near the door. "See if you can lift it with your mind."

It looks heavy, thought Bridgette, trying to trick Ms. Leadbetter into thinking she hadn't been practicing.

"Don't worry about how big it is," said Ms. Leadbetter. "Just try like you did with your pencil yesterday."

Bridgette nodded her head and focused on just one leg of the desk. After much concentration, the leg, and only the leg, rose from the brown rug about one inch before plopping back down to the floor. She let out a puff of air like she had seen George do and said, "It's too heavy."

"It's okay, Bridgette. You did quite well at this stage.

"George, let's see what you can do."

Without hesitation, George eyed the desk. His face turned red, and his cheeks were puffy. Suddenly, the desk began to rise slowly in the air.

After about four feet, Ms. Leadbetter said, "Now, hold it for 10 seconds right there."

With each passing second, George's face turned a darker shade of blue.

"Good, now gently let the desk drop back to the floor."

George exhaled a giant breath, one he had been holding the whole time, and the desk came crashing down to the floor.

The students, who had been focusing on their pencils, all jumped in their seats.

Ms. Leadbetter cringed and started writing on her clipboard. She must have been pressing down hard with her pen because of the loud scribbling it was making as she wrote. She stood and walked back to her podium and waited for the end of the class.

Just before the bell rang, Ms. Leadbetter addressed her students. "Class, you can stop your concentrating for now. I have something to tell you. Though it is rare and barely happens, (*yeah, right*) some students experience headaches in these sessions … not only here but also outside of the classroom. If this were to ever happen to you, please notify me at once so it can be remedied."

Bridgette heard Ms. Leadbetter's thoughts of *Yeah, right*. She glanced at Janice, who turned to look at her. Bridgette slowly shook her head. Janice nodded.

A red-haired girl with freckles raised her hand.

"Yes, Karen. What is it?" asked Ms. Leadbetter.

"Now that you mention it," she said, "I have been getting headaches. They started yesterday. They don't last for long and don't hurt much. Probably not even worth talking about, but I need this scholarship, so I want to make sure everything is done right."

"Thank you for your honesty, Karen." Ms. Leadbetter pulled her cell phone from her pocket and pushed a few buttons. She put the phone up to her ear and waited a few seconds. "We've got one."

What have I done, thought Karen. She started squirming in her chair.

Bridgette could read Karen's mind racing. She wanted to tell her everything but knew she couldn't, at least not in front of Ms. Leadbetter.

Moments later, the same nurse who had given them the shots walked through the door. All the students looked back, but Karen was the only one to stand from her chair. It wasn't a submissive stance; it was a panicky one.

"We have a runner!" shouted Ms. Leadbetter.

I have to get out of here, thought Karen. She dashed toward the nurse and shoved her out of the way. Grabbing the doorknob, she yanked open the door and rammed into Officer Halfpenny who was waiting on the other side.

"Hold on a minute," said Officer Halfpenny. His black hat tumbled to the floor, caused by the collision of the runaway student. Though his hair was cut short in the back and on the sides, his red bangs came flopping down toward his eyes. His light blue uniform was clean and pressed. "Where you think *you* goin'?" He grabbed her arms and held them tightly.

"Thank you, Officer Halfpenny," said Ms. Leadbetter. "I thought she was going to get away."

"No problem, ma'am," replied Officer Halfpenny. "Just tell me her ability so she can't use it on me befo I take her to get processed."

Ms. Leadbetter sighed. "She has no ability. She's a dud." She motioned with a flick of her hand. "Please, process away."

"You got it. Same arrangement as always?"

"Have I told you otherwise?" said Ms. Leadbetter, not expecting an answer.

He turned Karen toward the door while holding her arms behind her back. "Let's go, Red."

"No! I want to talk to my parents!" screamed Karen.

"They always say that," remarked Officer Halfpenny while he escorted Karen from the room.

The bell rang, and Ms. Leadbetter said, "George, please wait after class. I want to speak to you."

Bridgette gulped. She stood and walked toward him. Grabbing on his sleeve, she said, "Let's go."

George jerked his sleeve away from her with a hurt look on his face.

You're not my favorite person right now, he thought.

Bridgette read his mind and gave him a final pouty look and then smiled. She motioned with her head to follow her and kept walking.

Once outside the door, she met up with Janice. "He's not coming?" asked Janice.

"This is not good," said Bridgette. "What if we can't change the future? What if my visions are glimpses of what *will* happen and not what *could* happen?"

"I don't know," said Janice, "but we have other things to worry about." She tried to peek into the rectangular piece of glass in the center of the door.

"I hope he keeps his thoughts pure," said Bridgette. She walked down the hall. "Come on. Let's go to lunch. There's someone I want you to meet."

Janice gave her a sideways glare. "Is it that guy that's gonna kill me?"

"Why do you keep saying that?" said Bridgette. "How can you confuse saving with killing?"

Chapter 18

"Have a seat, George," ordered Ms. Leadbetter.

George had been standing in the back of the room, fidgeting nervously. He thought, *Which desk should I sit at?*

"Any desk is fine," said Ms. Leadbetter, answering his thoughts.

George slowly sat, easing his bottom on the chair like it might hurt if he sat down too fast.

"Tell me, George, have you been practicing your ability outside the classroom?"

Stunned by the question, George froze.

"I see. And what have you done?"

"What? I didn't say anything," said George nervously.

"You didn't have to."

"Can you read my mind?" asked George.

"What if I told you I could?"

"Then you would know that I wasn't using my ability outside the classroom."

"Then how do you explain your thoughts earlier when you said you couldn't wait to show me how strong you've gotten?"

Wow, you really can read minds, thought George.

"Yes, now answer my question."

"I don't know," said George. "I guess I just feel it. I just feel more powerful, more confident in my ability."

"I see." She stared at him with an untrusting scowl, as if she were waiting for him to slip up with one tiny word or thought.

"Can I go now?" begged George.

"One more thing before I let you leave," she responded. She held up her index finger.

George swallowed.

"Have you noticed any other unusual abilities? Perhaps something you've done? Or has anything happened to you that you can't really explain?"

George shook his head and answered honestly, "No."

"Dismissed."

He leapt from his chair and scooted for the door. Quickly, he opened it and ran into the hallway.

Again, Officer Halfpenny was waiting. "Whoa, where you think *you* going?" He grabbed George by the arm and pulled the door open. "Scuse me, ma'am, but do we need to process this one too?"

"No, Officer Halfpenny, and please do not show up at my door unless you have been summoned."

"Gotcha." He closed the door and let George's arm go. "Whatcha learning in there, boy?"

George didn't respond. He just raced down the hallway toward the cafeteria.

Once there, he grabbed a lunch and looked for a table.

The cafeteria was full of noisy students as usual. Hundreds of them swarmed the place, some sitting, others standing around, while still others were walking in or wandering out.

"George!" hollered Bridgette from his left. "Over here!"

He knew he had to make up with them sooner or later so he carried his tray with both hands and walked toward Bridgette and Janice, who were sitting at their own table. He stared at the burger on his tray while he walked.

"Have a seat, Whiz," said Janice when he approached.

George set his tray down. "You don't have to call me that."

"Is that a hint of humility I hear in your voice?" teased Janice.

"I'm glad you could join us, George," said Bridgette. "So, how did it go with Leadbetter?"

George pulled out a chair and sat down. "Don't worry. I didn't let her know anything about any of us. I told her I wasn't practicing outside of class."

"And she believed you?" asked Bridgette.

"I made sure not to have any stray thoughts that she could hear, and yes, she can definitely read minds. She read me like a book."

"Darn," said Bridgette, "I wish I could have been a fly on the wall in there so I could have heard how she talked to you. Then I could see if my vision came true or if it was altered. Can you tell me what she said?"

"Let's see. She asked me if I was using my ability anywhere else."

"Did she ask if *you* or anyone you *knew* was using their ability?" asked Bridgette with a serious tone.

"She definitely asked if *I* was using *my* ability," said George. "Why?"

"My vision was similar but a little bit different. I think we … *you* … changed the future."

"It could have gone a lot worse if you hadn't warned us all," admitted George.

"Georgie," said Janice, "that's twice you have been humble in the past couple of minutes. "What has gotten into you?"

"I had a talk with some good friends." George smiled at her.

Janice snarled and said, "Ugh."

"Speaking of good friends," said Bridgette. "Wouldn't you agree that you can never have too many of them?"

They both looked at Bridgette with a puzzled look. When they did, they noticed her standing and smiling. Wanda and her girls were standing at their table, trays in hand.

Janice stood from the table and clenched her fists and gritted her teeth. "Just because she's helping you doesn't mean we have to eat with you or look at your ugly mugs."

Wanda looked at Bridgette. "You didn't tell them?"

Bridgette smiled and shook her head. "Guys, this is Wanda, Maria, and Cathy. We're going to start eating together."

Janice sat back down. "How do you expect me to eat when the sight of that maggot makes me want to barf?"

"The feeling's mutual," replied Wanda. She sat down with her tray which held only a diet soda. "Sit down, girls."

Maria and Cathy placed their trays of diet sodas on the table and sat down on either side of their leader.

"Can I ask a question?" said George while looking at Wanda. "Why do you guys get trays when all you buy is diet soda? Wouldn't it be easier to just carry the can?"

"That was two questions," sneered Wanda, "and no, you can't ask a question."

"Counting questions *and* calories, I see," kidded George.

Wanda gave a fake smile, which vanished just as quickly as it had appeared. Then she leaned toward the middle of the table so all could hear. "Okay," she whispered, "we go tonight."

"Why tonight?" asked George. "That doesn't give us much time to plan and get stronger."

Wanda scowled at him. "If it was *your* sister, you'd want to go as quickly as you could."

"If it were *my* sister, she probably wouldn't have gotten caught," replied George.

"Do you even *have* a sister?" asked Wanda.

"Well," began George, "no, but-"

"I'm done talking to him," said Wanda rudely to Bridgette.

"I was there last night," said Janice. "Those dudes are wicked."

Wanda's eyes grew wide. "Did you see a small girl with a doll?"

"It was dark," answered Janice, "and I was being chased so I didn't have time to look around much."

"Sounds like you were scared," said Wanda.

Janice leaned her head toward Wanda. "I don't get scared," she said with her teeth gritted.

"I hope that's true," responded Wanda, "for my sister's sake."

Mention of Wanda's sister got Bridgette back to the task at hand. "So what do we do?"

"In order to get close enough," said Wanda, "you'll have to become a Berserker."

Bridgette cut in. "What do you mean *become* one?"

"What she means," said Maria, "is that you'll have to dress like them and act like them."

"Do you have any pics of them so I can see what I need to look like?" asked Bridgette.

"I'll help you," volunteered Janice. "I got a good look at them last night."

"Yeah, we both did," said George. "I can help as well."

"Great," said Wanda with fake excitement, "then you won't be needing us for anything."

"Wait a minute," said Bridgette. "How do we know what your little sister looks like?"

Wanda slid a wallet-sized photo across the table. "This was her three months ago."

Bridgette peeled the picture from the table and examined it. The girl looked like a miniature image of Wanda with long blonde hair except there was something quite different as well. She was missing teeth, of course, being only eight years of age, but that wasn't it either. Then it struck her; this girl was smiling. She was happy.

"Ahh, she looks just like you," cooed Bridgette.

Wanda scowled.

Without taking her eyes away from the picture, Bridgette asked, "What do we do when we get her?"

Wanda thought for a moment and then said, "My address is on the back, along with my cell number. Call me, and then we'll put her in the garage at my house."

"The garage?" said Bridgette.

"What can I say? We have a small house, and she was the one that wanted her bedroom out there."

Bridgette was still staring at her with her mouth hanging open.

Then Wanda added, "It's also where our game room is, so she cried until my parents gave in. I didn't care; I just wanted my own room."

Bridgette nodded and then said, "Uh, don't you think you'll want to let your parents know she's home?"

"Oh, I will," replied Wanda, "but I want it to be a surprise, and I don't want you chumps, I mean you *guys*, around when my parents see her."

Bridgette slid the picture in her back pocket. "I'll go tonight." She looked at George and Janice for their approval. After all, she needed them to help her disguise herself as a Berserker.

They nodded.

Wanda lifted her can of diet soda to her lips and finished it off. "Great, I'll keep my phone next to me the whole night." She stood from the table. "Ladies."

Cathy and Maria drank the rest of their drinks, placed their cans on their trays and also stood. With trays in hand, the three girls walked toward the entrance.

Bridgette looked at George. "George, can we meet at your house tonight?"

"Sure, how about eight o'clock? It'll be dark by then, and I'll have your disguise ready for you."

Bridgette looked at Janice.

"Are you sure you wanna do this?" asked Janice.

Bridgette smiled and nodded.

"I'll be there," groaned Janice.

Chapter 19

Confined in George's bedroom, Janice and George did their best to dress Bridgette up as a Berserker.

"I found these clothes at a thrift store after school today," said George. "It's amazing what five bucks can get you."

"I'll pay you back," said Bridgette.

"Nonsense," said George.

"I'm really liking the new George," said Bridgette. She looked at Janice for approval.

Janice shrugged her shoulders. "Could be worse."

Bridgette started dusting off her jeans with her hands.

"Don't do that," urged George. "I got them dirty on purpose. Same as your hooded jacket. They can't look too clean, or they might suspect you."

"This looks like an old army jacket with a hood," said Bridgette.

George nodded.

"Did they have another one?" asked Janice while admiring it.

George seemed to ignore the question as he said, "Okay, now put on the hood."

Janice folded her ponytail in half and raised the hood over her head.

"Perfect," said George. "Janice, what do you think?"

Janice headed for the door. "There's just one more thing. Follow me; I want to do the finishing touches."

They walked outside to George's mom's flower garden where varieties of colorful flowers grew next to the house. Janice reached down and picked up a handful of dirt. She rubbed it between her hands like it was soap. When she was done, she said to Bridgette, "Come here."

"I don't think I'm going to like this," said Bridgette. She crept up to Janice and closed her eyes.

Janice grabbed both sides of Bridgette's face and began smearing the dirt all over, including her forehead.

"Ewww!" cried Bridgette, "I hope there are no worms or bugs in this dirt."

"If there are," said George, "that might even help you blend in even more."

After getting Bridgette dirty, Janice leaned in as if she were going to kiss her.

Bridgette pulled her head back and said, "What are you doing?"

Janice sniffed. "Too clean. You smell too clean. Follow me." She pulled Bridgette's arm and led her to the trash can. Knowing exactly what was on Janice's mind, George ran ahead and lifted the lid. Janice tore open a plastic bag and dug her hand into the unknown. "Oh, this is disgusting. Whatever it is, it's wet and slimy, and it stinks bad."

Bridgette squeezed her eyes shut and said, "*Really?* Is this *really* necessary?"

Janice pulled Bridgette's hood off and plopped some of the smelly, rotten spaghetti-like substance on her head. "It's for your own protection." She couldn't help but laugh as she wiped her hands off on Bridgette's back.

Bridgette shook some of the icky stuff off her head and pulled her hood back on. *It's okay, it's for a good cause*, she thought.

"Okay," said George, "let's get going."

"Wait a minute," said Bridgette. "Where do you think *you're* going?"

George zipped up her jacket for her and said, "You didn't think we were going to let you go by yourself, did you?"

"I can't ask you guys to go with me," said Bridgette. "It's way too dangerous. There's no telling what these Berserkers will do to us if they catch us."

"We're going," said Janice forcefully, and that was the end of that.

Bridgette got a mischievous grin on her face. She reached into the garbage can and grabbed a squishy handful of spoiled food.

"Well, if you insist, then you'll need a bit of your own protection." She plopped the slimy goo on Janice's head.

It was totally out of character for Bridgette to do such a thing. Janice couldn't help but smile, and then they both started laughing.

When the laughter died down, they realized George would need to "freshen up" as well. They both looked in his direction.

George backpedaled a couple of steps. "Uh, maybe you guys won't need me after all."

The girls both reached into the garbage can and filled their hands with rotten food and trash.

"Get over here, George," commanded Janice. "We're in this together."

After George and Janice put on disguises, hooded jackets included, Janice led the way. "Come on; follow me."

George looked down at his jacket. Spoiled food was caked all over it and hanging from his hair. "I still say you guys got a bit carried away with my disguise."

Bridgette glanced at Janice and smiled. Janice kept her stern expression but was smiling on the inside.

They walked down the sidewalk in the cool dark night under the soft glow of street lights spaced out about every fifty yards. Cars were parked along both sides of the street. A couple of stray dogs trotted across the road, seemingly minding their own business. A traffic light turned red a few blocks away, and a car turned down the street, heading in their direction with its high beams on. Bridgette squinted at the car, trying to see who was driving. She couldn't see the driver, but she could tell it was an older car by the sound of the engine.

Just before the car reached them, it slowed down and stopped. The trio stopped walking and froze. They stared at the car, and the car with its high beams glared back at them.

Suddenly, a door opened.

George swallowed and looked on.

Bridgette concentrated on the door, waiting patiently.

Janice tightened her fists.

Hastily, a white cat was thrown out of the car. It meowed like it had been hurt during the toss out the door. The two dogs saw the cat and changed direction. Growling in a fit of rage, they charged the frightened cat, which scampered under a nearby car to hide.

Fits of laughter emanated from inside the car. A teenaged boy closed the door and stuck his head out of the rolled-down window. "Come on, pull up some. I wanna see those dogs chew that cat *up*."

The car edged forward. "Get 'em boys!"

The dogs, encouraged by the boy, seemed even more determined to make a meal out of the cat. They ran even faster. When they drew near the cat, it made a desperate run for it. With its little white legs it ran toward Bridgette.

Come here, kitty, thought Bridgette.

Like a deer being chased by a lion, the cat raced for its life toward Bridgette's safe arms.

Bridgette instinctively held her arms out as if to catch the cat in midair.

The cat made one final leap. Halfway to safety, the cat fell short of its goal. Just before reaching Bridgette's hands, one of the mutts tackled the poor thing. The two natural born enemies tangled and twisted to the ground. The cat hissed while the dog growled. They tore, bit, scratched, and clawed at each other. The cat was about to break free when the other dog, a bigger and uglier one tore into the fight. He grabbed the cat by the neck and started shaking its head. Five seconds later, and it was all over. The brownish black dog stood still, holding its dead prize in its mouth. The cat hung limp between its teeth. The other dog growled a few times and then sniffed the cat before biting into it a few times.

Once they were satisfied the cat was dead, the dogs released their clench on it, and it fell lifeless to the bloody sidewalk beneath it.

"Get!" screamed George. He raised his hands at the dogs to scare them away. It worked. They scampered off down the street to look for some more excitement.

"Woo hoo!" screamed the boy from inside the car. "Let's get out of here!"

The car revved its engine and peeled out down the street.

Bridgette, with her jaw hanging open and her arms still outstretched was speechless. Her head grew hot, and her body shook. She gritted her teeth together.

George walked up to her and said, "Are you okay, Bridge?"

Bridgette didn't say a word. She stared straight ahead while a vision began to form in her head. In the dream, she, George, and Janice were standing in a residential neighborhood at someone's brick house. Another person, smaller in stature, was with them, but she couldn't see her face; her back was to her. They walked into a garage and entered a dimly lit room. Wanda greeted them. Janice shoved the person toward her and said something, but Bridgette couldn't make it out, mainly because Janice was talking to her in the present, snapping her out of her futuristic vision.

"Bridgette, are you okay?" asked Janice while shaking her on the shoulder.

Bridgette blinked a couple of times and said, "What? Did you say something?"

"Yeah, we should keep moving," replied Janice.

Bridgette gazed down at the lifeless cat. "I can't believe there are people in this world that are that cruel." She crinkled her eyebrows.

"Hey, you had a vision, didn't you?" asked Janice.

Bridgette nodded. "I think we were at Wanda's house. My guess is that we had her sister with us, but for some strange reason you were kind of mean to her."

George spoke up. "Did you get a good look at me? I mean, did you notice any blood on my face or clothes? Was I hurt?"

"I didn't look that closely, George. I didn't have enough time. Someone snapped me out of my vision." She looked back at Janice.

"Sorry, for acting like I cared," said Janice.

"Thank you for caring, Janice," said Bridgette. "I appreciate you so much, but I think from now on, if you guys see me in a trance, let me finish the vision on my own so that I can get a good glimpse into the future. It might prove to be quite helpful. Who knows? It could even save our lives."

"Let's not get too dramatic," said Janice. "I said I was sorry, so let's just drop it and keep moving."

"You've already been forgiven, Janice," said Bridgette. She smiled and followed the others. "Oh, don't let me forget, Janice. After we get Wanda's sister, if there's time, I can introduce you to that guy."

"Who is he?" cried Janice.

"You'll see," said Bridgette.

"Does George know him?" she asked.

Bridgette glanced at George. "I believe he does."

George tried to join the conversation. "I do?"

Bridgette walked out in front. "Come on; let's hurry and get this over with."

When they reached the dark alley, Janice said, "This is it. You two stay behind me. We need to find this Alpha guy."

"No matter what happens tonight," said Bridgette, "I just want to say thank you to both of you for coming out here with me. It means a lot."

"Okay," said Janice, "enough of the sobby speeches. Let's go show this Alpha his omega."

"Hey," said George, "that was pretty witty."

With Janice in the lead, the three walked away from the dimly lit street and into the alley where the darkness swallowed them whole.

Just as before, Janice saw the orange light ahead from the glowing trash barrel. "I can see 'em," she whispered. "Don't look them in the eyes."

"Why?" whispered Bridgette.

"Because their eyes are bloodshot, and yours aren't. They might figure out that you're not one of them."

Bridgette adjusted her hood and stared down at the ground. George and Janice did the same. They slowed their walks as if they had no real destination, only to appear wandering aimlessly.

Gusts of wind were blowing dirt and debris throughout the darkened alley. The flames in the barrel were dancing frantically like they were angry and wanted to jump out at anyone who dared to get too close.

Trying to blend in, they circled around the barrel alongside some of the Berserkers. Janice reached her hands out toward the flames. She kept her mouth shut this time. George and Bridgette copied her movements.

Slowly, Bridgette lifted her eyes. With her hood pulled over her head and mostly across her face as well, her eyes were hidden in the darkened shadows. She could see the nearby faces of the Berserkers. They were all just kids! Some had faces that were scarred up while others were merely dirty. All of them had sunken white eyes with blood vessels running throughout.

Everything was so weird and foreign to Bridgette. It was like she was visiting a third-world country or something. So when she heard a sneeze coming from the darkness, it kind of startled her because she didn't expect Berserkers to have any human qualities left.

The sneezer stepped closer to the fire. The flames painted some light on her face, just enough to tell that it was Wanda's sister. Her once beautiful long blonde hair was all knotted up. Dirty tears were etched into her cheeks. Her clothes were ragged and torn. She wasn't tied up or anything. She was walking around freely, no one stopping her from doing whatever she wanted.

Bridgette looked down and thought, *How can she be a hostage if she's not even being forced to stay? This doesn't add up. Perhaps she knows she can't outrun the Berserkers. Or perhaps...* Bridgette lifted her eyes once more to get a better look at the girl. *Look up,* she thought. She tried to read the girl's mind. Nothing. Not able to get a full look at the girl, Bridgette resorted to using her ability. Carefully, and with not too much power, she willed the girl to raise her head just enough for what she needed. While her head raised, Bridgette could see the reflection of the flames in the girl's white bloodshot eyes. Her hunch was right. Wanda's sister was one of them. She had become a Berserker.

Chapter 20

Slowly, Bridgette slid to her left until she bumped into Janice, who ever so slightly turned her head to see what she wanted. Bridgette nodded at Wanda's sister.

Janice thought in her head, *Is that her?*

Bridgette nodded very carefully.

But she's one of them, thought Janice.

Bridgette nodded again.

Then let's get out of here. There's nothing we can do, thought Janice.

Bridgette shook her head slowly. She had told Wanda she was going to get her sister back, and that's exactly what she intended to do.

Well, then what should I do? Do you want me to grab her? asked Janice?

Bridgette nodded.

George was too far from Bridgette's reach so she concentrated and lifted George a few inches off the ground and dropped him. That got his attention.

George turned his head toward Bridgette, a little faster than he should have. It was a sudden movement, something Berserkers were not known for. He drew the attention of a couple of the Berserkers near the fire.

The two Berserkers walked slowly up to him and started sniffing him like dogs. One of them got right in his face and tried to stare him in the eyes.

George squeezed his eyes shut. *Bridgette, help me,* he thought, knowing she would be able to hear his thoughts.

"Now!" screamed Bridgette.

Janice grabbed Wanda's sister and threw her over her shoulder like a fireman's carry. Next she started running down the alley toward the street from which they came. Wanda's sister started kicking and screaming. She pounded on Janice's back with her defiant fists. While trying to control the little girl's legs and run at the same time, Janice was unaware of the Berserker she was running toward. After about 15 long strides, she ran into what felt like a brick wall. Wanda's sister tumbled to the ground. Janice staggered like a drunkard. The Berserker had clobbered her with an arm directly across her face. Janice cleared her head and tried to focus in the darkness. She squinted until she could make out the figure.

"Karen, is that you?" asked Janice.

The long red-haired girl from their Mind over Matter class had struck a crushing blow. She didn't say anything, only swung again, but this time Janice was ready for it. She ducked out of the way.

Janice's adrenaline started pumping now. She squeezed her fists together. Obviously, the time for talking was over, and she was fine with that. She preferred to speak with her hands anyway.

Over by the flaming barrel, the two Berserkers had ahold of George. It looked like they were making a wish on a wishbone. One pulled one direction while the other was pulling in the opposite. George shook his arms and screamed his head off while trying to break free.

All of the noise only attracted more of the Berserkers. They came running like someone had just rung the dinner bell.

Bridgette calmly lifted her hand in the air, and George rose over 10 feet off the ground. The two Berserkers lost their grip on him and tried jumping up high to reach him again. This gave Bridgette a free moment to look around and see what was going on. She noticed Janice fighting off Karen and seemed to be holding her own. Still, she thought she should help so they could grab Wanda's sister and get out of there before things got worse.

In midair and out of danger, George was able to think more clearly. Seeing the blaze flickering in the barrel gave him an idea. He focused on the flames and flicked his fingers toward a nearby Berserker. The fire leaped out of the barrel and struck a Berserker's shirt. Quickly, it started crawling up his sleeve and down his back. The Berserker screamed and fell to the ground, rolling around in the dirt like a dog taking a dirt bath.

While continuing to hold George off the ground with one hand, Bridgette moved forward toward Janice. She was only able to take two steps before she had her breathing cut off. A gigantic hand clamped onto her neck from behind. Calmly, she stared at the pair of legs behind her and caused the legs to lift off the ground. She pushed backward with her feet while at the same time releasing her mental grip on the legs. Whoever it was collapsed to the ground instantly with Bridgette falling backwards on top of him. It knocked the wind right out of him. She rolled across the limp body. It was the Alpha, at least it fit the description of the Alpha. His hair was long, dark, and tangled. He lay there on the ground wearing a dirty white t-shirt and jeans. His muscles rippled underneath his tight shirt. She gazed down at his large hands. There was dirt under his fingernails. His chest was heaving up and down. Slowly, he started crawling to his feet while trying to catch his breath.

"George!" yelled Bridgette. "Let's get out of here!" She ran toward Janice and motioned with her hand in the air for George to follow. It was like she was flying a kite without the string. She turned back to Janice. "Grab the girl, and let's go."

"Uh, it's kind of hard to do two things at once," replied Janice. Just then she dodged another swing from Karen.

Solving Janice's problem, Bridgette focused and flew George into Karen's body. They crashed to the ground.

Wanda's sister was sitting against a wall with her arms wrapped around her knees. Janice ran over and grabbed her again and hoisted her onto her shoulders like before. Luckily, she didn't fight it this time. Perhaps she knew there was no one left to help her.

Luckily, George had kicked Karen in the face when he landed on her. It knocked her out cold. He picked himself up off the ground and raced with the others out of the alley. It was an eerie sound, hearing only their footsteps in the night, clomping in the dirt as they ran to safety.

When they reached the lit street, they stopped and turned toward the alley. They couldn't see or hear anyone coming. Janice put the girl down but kept a firm hold of her arm.

Bridgette peered at Janice and said, "Looks like Karen really gave you a good punch in the eye."

Janice's eye was already swelling up from where Karen had smacked her with her arm.

"Well, if it weren't for this little Berserker here, she wouldn't have been able to sucker punch me." She glared down at Wanda's sister.

"It's not *her* fault," said Bridgette. "Let's not forget who is responsible for all of this."

"You mean Wanda?" asked Janice. She put her hand on her temple and moaned.

"No, Ms. Leadbetter, of course," replied Bridgette. "Are you having another headache?"

Janice closed her eyes. "Yeah, and this one hurts a lot."

"Karen was just in class, and now she's already out here," said Bridgette. "I think it's safe to say you don't have much time. Let's hurry and drop Wanda's sister off so that I can introduce you to *that guy* right after."

"Is he a doctor?" asked Janice.

"He's definitely a healer," she responded.

"Anything to avoid turning into one of *these* things," said Janice while looking down at Wanda's sister.

They followed all of the street lights to Wanda's house. It was getting late, and Wanda's sister seemed to stagger as she walked, almost as if she would fall asleep at any moment. Bridgette had texted Wanda to let her know they were coming.

They turned down Wanda's street, a richer part of town. The houses were all made of bricks and had two stories. Even the trees and bushes looked to be worth a lot of money the way they had been groomed and well kept.

When they reached Wanda's garage, they tapped on the door. Wanda opened it, and they slowly walked into the dimly lit room. Once inside, the garage door closed electronically.

Janice shoved the little girl toward her sister and said, "Here she is."

Wanda dropped to her knees and embraced her. "Sissy, you're alive."

Sissy just stood there like a rag doll.

"I think now I know why you wanted us to bring her to the garage," replied Bridgette. "You knew all along that she was a Berserker, didn't you?"

"Well, would you have saved her if I told you she was?" said Wanda snidely.

"Again, you question my motives," said Bridgette. "If you would take the time to get to know me, you would see that I am not that kind of person. I help my friends. I don't try to see what's in it for me."

"As I recall, that's exactly how we got all this started," said Wanda. "Remember, you had conditions in order to help me. We have to eat with you in the cafeteria so you don't look like a bunch of losers."

"Are you kidding me?" said Bridgette. "We're eating together so that we can get to know each other better and become friends. I not only tried to help you save your sister, but I was trying to save *you* as well."

"Save me from what?"

"From yourself," replied Bridgette. "You need guidance."

"What about *her*?" said Wanda. She had nodded at Janice and her swollen black eye. "She's no different than me. Where's her *guidance*?"

Bridgette's jaw dropped. "Do you even know how she got that black eye? She got it by rescuing your sister. She didn't have to help me tonight, but she wanted to."

Wanda swallowed. "Oh, thank you ... I guess."

"Don't bother; I did it for Bridgette, not for you," replied Janice rudely.

"You see?" whined Wanda.

"We're working on it," replied Bridgette. "We all need guidance sometimes. In fact, I'm introducing Janice to someone tonight to help her. Care to join us?"

"I can't. As you can see, I have family matters to attend to."

"You're right," agreed Bridgette. "How insensitive of me. I apologize. You see; nobody's perfect."

"I don't know why you care so much," said Wanda, almost spitting it out of her mouth.

"Well, don't give up on me," said Bridgette, "because I'm not giving up on you."

Janice looked at Wanda. "Disgustingly sweet, isn't she? Makes me wanna barf, but hey, we've all got our issues."

They walked to the exit.

"We'll see you at school tomorrow at lunch," said Bridgette while they walked out the door.

"So that's it?" said George. "We just hand her off like a baton and leave?"

"You heard her," said Bridgette. "She's got family matters to attend to, and I don't want to interfere with that."

"But we went through all that trouble, and for what?" said George.

Bridgette turned around and looked George in the eyes. "Come on, George, you can't be serious. We just reunited a girl with her family."

"Uh, she's not a girl anymore," corrected George. "She's a Berserker."

"This is what Wanda wanted," replied Bridgette. "Now, hopefully, we will have gained her trust and maybe even her friendship. I don't think she'll be messing with us in our dreams anymore."

"She better not," said Janice in a threatening tone while clenching her fists.

"Come on, Janice," said Bridgette, "it's time to meet the person who's going to save your life."

Chapter 21

When they reached Bridgette's house, George walked home. Bridgette and Janice walked into Bridgette's bedroom and closed the door.

"So where is he?" asked Janice.

Bridgette walked over to the small nightstand near the head of her bed. She picked up a thick book that looked pretty worn and said, "He's right here."

"What?" Janice looked confused.

"Don't worry," assured Bridgette, "you don't have to read the whole book, although you may want to later. Just focus on the New Testament."

"The new what?" asked Bridgette, looking overwhelmed and irritated. "This says Holy Bible."

"Here, let me show you." Bridgette grabbed the Bible and opened it to the latter half of the book. "See, just start with Matthew, and then look for all the words that are typed in red. That's him: Jesus."

"I thought you already knew that I wasn't in to this religious stuff."

"Do you want to become a Berserker?" asked Bridgette.

"No, but-"

"Then read His words in red," interrupted Bridgette. "You will not find wisdom like that anywhere. Try to read, at least, Matthew, Mark, Luke, and John. It will change your life, which is what you need right now."

"What's He going to tell me?"

"It's different for everyone," answered Bridgette.

"Huh?" said Janice. "Do the words change or something?"

"What I mean is, you can read it several times and usually come away with something new to apply to your life."

"I don't see what the big deal is, but I'll do it," said Janice. "Seems like I'm running out of time." She closed her eyes and winced from another wave of pain in her head.

"Read it tonight," urged Bridgette. "At least read Matthew, and then practice moving your pencil again."

"These headaches are starting to happen more often, and they hurt more too." She held the Bible close to her body and headed for the door.

"I'll be praying for you," said Bridgette.

She walked her to the front door of the house and watched her start walking home.

"Stay away from the alley!" called out Bridgette.

Without turning around, Janice raised her arm high in the air as if to say, "I got it covered."

Bridgette kissed her parents goodnight and went to bed.

While lying in the darkness, she put her hands behind her head and stared up at the ceiling. She couldn't sleep: too many things on her mind. Thoughts of Berserkers infiltrated her brain.

Hours later, while wondering how Wanda and her family were getting along, Bridgette finally nodded off. Instantly, she dreamt she was at Wanda's house. She found herself standing in Wanda's room, staring at Wanda sleeping. With her mind, she yanked the covers off of her.

In her purple pajamas, Wanda sat up in her bed. "What are you doing here?" she asked.

"Very funny," said Bridgette. "As if you didn't just summon me into one of your dreams. I thought you weren't going to do this anymore."

"Uh, I was sleeping, duh," said Wanda rudely. "You're the one who woke *me* up."

"Well, if you didn't pull me into one of your dreams, then …" She thought for a few seconds. "*I* pulled *you* into one of *my* dreams?"

"Wait," said Wanda, "let me see if I can fly." She sat on her bed and concentrated, but nothing happened. "Nope."

Bridgette floated in the air, and just to show off, she juggled eight different books from Wanda's bookcase, without even looking at them.

"How are you doing this?" asked Wanda.

"I don't know," answered Bridgette. "I guess I have *your* powers now too."

A tear rolled down Wanda's cheek.

"What's wrong?" asked Bridgette. "Where's your sister?"

"Sissy's gone again. I went to the bathroom, and when I came out, the front door was open, and she was gone."

"Did you try to find her, you know, in her dreams?"

"I tried, but you have to be asleep," replied Wanda. "If your target isn't asleep, it doesn't work."

"Maybe I can try," said Bridgette. "I'll try to take us both to her."

Bridgette closed her eyes and thought about Sissy. Seconds later they were both in the dark alley with the fiery barrel. Sissy was right in front of them, the Alpha standing next to her with his hood on.

The Alpha, widened his bloodshot eyes and then lunged at the girls.

Bridgette held out her hand and froze him like a statue. "Not so fast, Alpha."

He reached out with his dirty hands and tried grabbing at the girls, grunting all the while but to no avail.

"Don't waste your strength," said Bridgette calmly. "I'm not going to hurt you."

The Alpha responded to Bridgette's calm voice by dropping his arms and relaxing.

"Good," said Bridgette.

"Wow, it's like you calmed the savage beast," said Wanda.

"Shhh," hushed Bridgette, "I don't want to scare him or get him angry." She looked him squarely in the eyes and said, "Why have you taken Sissy again?"

To this question the Alpha became irate. He didn't seem to like the accusation. He grunted some more and tried reaching for the girls again.

Bridgette then heard his thoughts. *I didn't take her. She came back to me using her own free will.*

"But why?" asked Bridgette. "Why would she want to come back here instead of live with her family at home?"

"Uh, excuse me," interrupted Wanda. "Are you talking to me or to him?"

"Oh, sorry," apologized Bridgette, "I'm speaking to him. I can read his mind."

Wanda's eyes bulged while she looked at Bridgette in disbelief.

"Why?" asked Bridgette again.

The Alpha took a few deep breaths. *Why don't you ask the girl?*

Bridgette turned toward Sissy. Her long blonde hair looked ratty and tangled in the flickering firelight. "Why did you come back here?"

This is my new home, replied Sissy with her thoughts. *I belong here.*

"You belong with your parents at home. You're just a kid," said Bridgette.

I'm a freak. I don't want anyone to see me, especially my parents. Tears streamed down her cheeks. She reached up with the back of her hand and wiped them away.

"What if I can help you?" asked Bridgette.

How?

Bridgette thought for a moment and then said, "I don't know just yet, but when the time comes, will you let me help you, all of you?" She glanced at the Alpha.

He nodded.

"Okay, take care of her," said Bridgette, talking now to the Alpha.

"Wait, we're leaving her here?" asked Wanda.

"She doesn't want to go home," said Bridgette. "She thinks she's a freak."

"She has to come home with me," demanded Wanda, walking toward her sister.

Bridgette clutched her arm and stopped her. "First of all, this is just a dream. Secondly, let her stay. She's safe here. No one bothers them. You can bring her food and clothing if you're worried about her. We have to find out what's going on so we can help them get back to normal."

"You think that's possible?" asked Wanda with a glimmer of hope in her voice.

"*All* things are possible," declared Bridgette.

Wanda felt a surge of happiness flow through her body, brought about by Bridgette's confidence. It was the first time she had felt happy in a long time. Through joyful tears and a half-smile she managed to say, "Did you hear that, Sis? We're gonna help you get better." She reached out to hug her sister.

Sissy grunted and retreated back behind the barrel of fire.

Not to be outdone, the Alpha growled and tried to lunge at Wanda, but Bridgette still had his legs frozen.

Wanda held her hands out and said, "It's okay. I understand. You don't like to be touched. Let me just remind you that this is not just an ordinary dream." She looked at Bridgette. "We need to do something so that when they wake up, they will know that we were really here."

"Like what?" asked Bridgette.

"I'm afraid we're going to have to do something they will *feel* in the morning, and since this is *your* dream world, it's gonna have to be done by you."

"You want me to hurt them?" asked Bridgette in disbelief.

"It's gotta be done," replied Wanda.

"Well," thought Bridgette aloud, "it does seem logical, given the circumstances."

She allowed the Alpha to retreat back to the barrel of fire next to Sissy.

Once he reached her, Bridgette said, "I'm really sorry for what I'm about to do, but I need to make sure you remember this dream when you wake up. I need you to remember that it's more than a dream, not just something you made up in your heads."

Bridgette swallowed and said, "Forgive me, Jesus." She focused on Sissy's and the Alpha's hands, one of each. Slowly and shakily, their hands moved over the flames inside the barrel. Sissy screamed first while the flames sizzled against her skin. The Alpha took longer, but eventually he groaned while the flames licked his knuckles and made them crispy.

107

"I'm sorry," cried Bridgette. Tears gushed from her eyes. She fell to her knees and stared at the ground.

The searing pain angered the Alpha. He started sprinting toward Bridgette in a mad rage.

Bridgette held up one hand and shouted, "Wake up!"

The Alpha and Sissy both turned to vapor and disappeared.

"Where'd they go?" asked Wanda.

"I woke them from their nightmare," said Bridgette. Tears were dripping off her nose and tickling her skin.

The more she thought about what she had done, the angrier she became with Ms. Leadbetter. After all, it was her teacher's fault that there were Berserkers in the world.

Bridgette looked skyward. She cried more openly now almost in convulsions. Her face grew hotter than a branding iron. She wanted to scream, and scream she did. One word was able to escape her lips, one word that rose high above the sound of the crackling fire in the nearby barrel. "Whyyyyyyyyyy!!!"

The injustice of it all was almost too much for her to bare, but something good was going to come from it. She braced herself for the futuristic vision that was entering her head.

Chapter 22

Staring off into the darkness, images began to form in Bridgette's mind. She and George were sitting in a classroom, no other students around. Ms. Leadbetter was there too, standing behind a podium as usual wearing a navy blue business suit.

She cleared her throat. "Did you two really think you had me fooled?" She was glaring directly at Bridgette.

George and Bridgette looked at each other and swallowed.

"I've known what you two were up to for quite some time now."

"Exactly what is it that you think we've been up to?" asked Bridgette innocently.

"Don't be coy with me," warned Ms. Leadbetter while pointing at Bridgette. "The question you should be asking is *What do I do to you now, now that you know that I know what you're up to.*"

Ms. Leadbetter looked at the door that led to the hallway. "Nurse Meyers!"

The nurse, dressed in her white uniform, opened the door with a needle in her hand. Carefully, she held it upright while she walked into the room toward Ms. Leadbetter.

The door closed behind her, but not before Officer Halfpenny stepped into the room and blocked it with his body. He looked at Bridgette and George and pointed at them. While shaking his finger, he said, "I knowed that I would see you two again. I just knowed it."

"Ahhh, Nurse Meyers," began Ms. Leadbetter, "thank you for coming. I see you have our little surprise with you."

George started shaking at his desk. He glanced at Bridgette who merely slowly shook her head at him.

Ms. Leadbetter grinned at George. "George!"

The mere mention of his name from Ms. Leadbetter's shrill voice caused him to jump in his seat.

She continued. "I'm going to give you the option. Shall I inject this into *you*, or should I inject it into your friend?"

Nurse Meyers walked between the two students and waited for directions.

George gazed over at Bridgette. His eyes glowed, and a tear raced down his cheek. *What should I do?* he thought to Bridgette.

Bridgette didn't do or say anything.

"Wh what's in it?" asked George.

"Curious little thing," aren't you," snapped Ms. Leadbetter. "I suppose this means you choose yourself so you can find out what it is."

"Give it to me!" cried out Bridgette bravely.

Ms. Leadbetter glanced at George. "I didn't hear *you* say that, George. Is that what you want?"

George looked at Bridgette. She nodded to him.

"Yes," he replied. "That's what I want."

"Good," said Ms. Leadbetter wickedly, "then we'll give it to you anyway. Did you actually think I was going to let you choose? How naïve of you." She chuckled a few times then gave Nurse Meyers the go-ahead nod.

Nurse Meyers rolled up George's sleeve

George squeezed his eyes together. "No! My mom's going to be upset, and I know she wouldn't approve of this."

Ms. Leadbetter reached behind the podium and pulled out a piece of paper. "Don't forget, Georgie, we have your parent's consent." She waved the paper at him.

Bridgette stood from her chair.

"Bridgette, did you hear me?" asked Wanda, snapping her out of her vision.

"Wanda, what did you do that for?"

"Do what?" replied Wanda. "I'm just talking to you."

"Ugh, you're right," agreed Bridgette. She didn't feel like explaining that she could see into the future. It's bad enough that Wanda knew about her being able to read minds.

"Well, I guess you can get me out of your dream now," said Wanda.

"Agreed," said Bridgette. "See you tomorrow at lunch?"

"Sure."

The next day at school before they met in Mind over Matter class, Bridgette had explained everything to George. She told how she could control dreams just like the Dream Weavers, how Wanda's sister, Sissy, had gone back to the Berserkers, and how she had the vision of the future event involving him and Ms. Leadbetter.

While standing in the hallway outside their Mind over Matter class, Bridgette asked George, "Have you seen Janice?"

"Nope." A worried look appeared on his face. "You don't suppose she-"

"Don't even say it," commanded Bridgette. "She probably stayed up all night reading the Bible, and now she's overslept."

"The whole Bible?" asked George.

"No, silly, just part of the New Testament for now."

"But why?" asked George. "Are you trying to save her soul before she becomes a Berserker?"

"Not exactly," replied Bridgette. "You see, I have this theory."

George looked interested. "Go on."

"Well, what I believe - and I could be wrong, but I don't think so - I think that the shot they gave us only works on *nice* people. The nicer you are, the stronger you become."

George took it in and thought about it for a moment. "Makes sense, and I would agree with you except for one thing."

"What's that?"

"Ms. Leadbottom. She's not nice. At. All."

"I think that can be explained as well," said Bridgette. "What if she once *was* nice when she was originally given the shot?"

"That's a big *what if*," said George. "I think it's a bit much to believe too. That woman is wicked through and through. I can't image her *ever* being nice."

"I disagree," said Bridgette. "Though we're all born sinners, I think we still have a lot of goodness in us until we've been

111

misguided." Bridgette shook her head. "No . . . I think something devastating happened to that woman, something so horrible that it caused her to cross over to the dark side."

"But how can you be so sure?" asked George. "You're such a good person. You believe in everyone. Maybe your own goodness is clouding your judgment."

"I've always been a good judge of character," said Bridgette, "and I believe I'm right in this instance too."

"So *that's* why you have Janice reading the Bible," said George.

Bridgette nodded. "She doesn't have time to learn to be nice; she needs it to happen quickly."

"It'll take a miracle," said George with little hope.

Bridgette smiled. "Then we sent her to the right place.

"Come on, let's go to class. We can check on Janice after school today."

Chapter 23

Twenty years ago

"We did it!" cried Professor Leadbetter.

"A toast," said his wife.

Dressed in white lab coats, they clinked little test tubes together, tubes filled with a glowing orange liquid. They put the tubes to their lips and tilted their heads back, emptying the contents completely into their mouths.

After swallowing the bitter liquid and making a prune face, Professor Leadbetter said, "We've got to come up with a better way to administer this stuff."

"That's exactly what I've done," said his wife. "I have created a more potent dose that can be given intravenously." She held up another test tube that had a stopper on one end to prevent the orange liquid from spilling out while she shook it back and forth with her fingers.

"I knew there was a reason I married you," said Professor Leadbetter kiddingly. "And I know just the person we can try it out on."

"Who?"

"Jane, of course," replied the professor.

"*Our* Jane?" asked his wife. "But, she's our only daughter, our only child."

"Precisely," said Professor Leadbetter. "We already know this stuff works so let's give the more powerful dose to our daughter. She'll be the strongest of all of us. She is the future. She is *our* future."

"Hold still, Jane, you're only going to feel a pinch." Professor Leadbetter pinched the back of his daughter's arm and poked the needle in carefully.

"Ouch!"

His eyes widened while the orange liquid plunged into her skin and disappeared. He handed the empty syringe to his wife. "There, that wasn't that bad, was it?"

Jane's once pleasant face was teary eyed and full of anguish. "What have you done to me, Daddy?" She turned her head. "Why, Mom?"

Her mother grabbed her and hugged her tightly. "We thought you'd want this."

Jane shook her head and bawled into her mother's chest.

"Ahhh, she'll get over it once she starts developing her abilities," said her dad.

***

"Dad, I made my pencil move today!" shouted Jane.

"That's great, honey," replied her father. He was writing down notes from his latest experiment. *Now leave me alone so I can get my work done.*

"What did you say?"

"Huh?" Her dad put down his pen. "I said that's great."

Jane shook her head like maybe she had imagined reading her father's thoughts. She left the study and walked down the hallway toward the kitchen.

"Mom," she called, "guess what I can do."

Her mom was washing dishes and had bubbles all over her hands while she dipped them into the sink full of soapy water. "You moved the pencil today?"

"Yes, isn't it great?" said Jane.

"It sure is," replied her mom. She flashed a quick smile, and then it quickly disappeared. *What would be great is if you would leave me alone for a few minutes so I can get some work done.*

Shocked at what she heard her mother thinking, Jane left the kitchen and meandered into her bedroom. She fell on her bed and thought about her new abilities.

While the days passed, Jane soon learned what her parents really thought of her. She felt like she was not wanted. They would say one thing but think another. It soon became evident that they didn't even love her. For twelve years they had fooled her into thinking they cared about her, but it was all a sham. They were too in love with their work to ever love anything else, especially a daughter who was always in the way or hindering their progress on their latest experiments.

When she ran away, she thought it would be for just a day or two. Maybe then her parents would miss her and realize how much they loved her.

The days ticked by like seconds. Night after night she would watch the local news on TV at the mall in one of the stores that sold televisions. Not once did she see a picture of herself on the screen as a missing person. Her parents had simply not cared enough to even search for her.

Feeling miserable and without a family, Jane caught a bus and escaped to Nevada. California would no longer be her home.

The bus dropped her off in Las Vegas. It didn't take long for the police to find her ditching school. She never spoke a word to them. She pretended that she couldn't talk. With no identification and without saying a word, no one would be able to figure out where she came from.

Eventually, she was dropped into the foster system where a man and woman seemed to have taken pity on her and tried to adopt her.

"Isn't she the cutest little thing?" said her soon-to-be mother.

"She'll do," replied the woman's husband.

The woman spoke to the case worker in the office where they officially picked Jane up. "Now when should we expect to receive our first check for her, uh, expenses?"

"You should receive it by the third of each month, starting next month. How many foster children do you have now anyway?"

"This will be lucky number seven," replied the woman. "We just love children."

When they reached their van, the man and woman seemed to change their demeanor. The woman shoved Jane through the doorway of the van and said, "Get in there, sweetie. You're gonna make us an extra eight hundred bucks a month."

Is that all I am to you? thought Jane.

Jane didn't say anything, however; she wanted to keep her silence so no one would find out that she was a runaway. Anything was better than living with those non-loving people she thought were her parents.

Jane soon discovered that the eight hundred dollars a month was not all they wanted her for. They also needed someone else to help clean up around the house. Seven kids of all ages made daily messes that needed to be cleaned up.

What had her life become? One day she was living fine with both parents, oblivious to how they felt about her, but still, she was content. Now she found herself living with complete strangers who were collecting money to take care of her but never spent a penny on her. Not only that, but she was treated like a slave as well.

She decided that people just couldn't be trusted, not her parents, surely not her foster parents, not the police who sent her to the foster system in the first place, and certainly not any of the kids that seemed to tease her wherever she went because of her refusal to speak. It was around this time she realized her abilities stopped getting stronger. She held onto the powers she had obtained in California with her parents, but that was all. She never weakened; she just stayed the same.

After a miserable year with her foster parents, she ran away again. With luck she was able to find an empty home owned by the bank that no one wanted to buy. She took down the "for sale" sign and broke in through the back door.

Until she was old enough to work, she used her mind-reading ability to prey on people who felt sorry for her. She always dressed like a homeless person for this reason. Once she knew they were feeling sorry for her, she would ask them for money, food, or clothing.

She thought of these people who helped her as suckers. In *her* mind, there were two kinds of people in the world: suckers and users, and she didn't like either of them.

She was bitter and planned on staying that way. She figured if her own parents couldn't love her, then no one could. Love was just a word people used to get what they wanted. It surely wasn't anything a person could actually feel or express.

Chapter 24

Bridgette and George walked into the Mind over Matter classroom and sat down next to each other as there was no real seating chart. Every time the door opened, they would quickly turn their heads to see if it was Janice, but it never was.

After the bell rang, Ms. Leadbetter took role, and before she could start the class session, Bridgette raised her hand.

"Yes, Bridgette," called Ms. Leadbetter.

"Did Janice call in sick today?"

"I don't know, but I wouldn't pay too much attention to it," she replied. "Students have a longstanding reputation of dropping out of my class, especially when they don't develop the abilities that you and George are experiencing." She looked around the room. There were only five students present. "As you can see, students are dropping like flies, and-"

"What happened to Karen?" asked Bridgette, cutting her off.

Ms. Leadbetter glared daggers at Bridgette. "I'm sorry, did you have something to say that was more important than what *I* was just saying?"

Bridgette covered her mouth with her hand. She pulled her fingers away from her lips to speak. "I'm terribly sorry. The thought just kind of popped into my mind and rolled right out of my mouth."

The anger leapt out of Ms. Leadbetter's eyes, and she said, "Yes, well, let's not let that happen again . . . if you know what's good for you."

What's that supposed to mean? thought Bridgette.

She realized her mistake right after her thought was finished. It wasn't just her thinking it though. She could read the minds of the other students as well, but she should have known better than to think her mind around Ms. Leadbetter.

Ms. Leadbetter calmly walked toward the whiteboard and grabbed the yardstick. She squeezed it until the whites of her knuckles showed. Fiercely, she swung it so hard at a desk that when it made contact, it splintered into pieces. "If you are all wondering what I meant by saying 'if you know what's good for you,' let me explain. I can make your life here miserable, not just here, but also at your house, the house that the school has provided for you and your family. Would you like me to call your parents and explain to them why they must pack up and move? That it was all because of their spoiled little brat of a child?"

Nobody said a word. They didn't dare.

Ms. Leadbetter's face, that had twisted and contorted during her power posturing, had snapped back into shape.

"I didn't think so.

"Now, let's move on to more pressing business. Who is having headaches?"

The students gulped and looked around the room to signify that it wasn't them, but perhaps someone else in the room was having them.

The wicked teacher looked at a boy with stubbly brown hair who was sitting in the front row and said, "David, you seem awfully quiet today. What seems to be the matter?"

David cleared his throat nervously. "Um, I'm always quiet, Ms. Leadbetter; we all are. We know you don't like speaking in your classroom."

"You are correct, David," said Ms. Leadbetter; "however, there is one thing you failed to realize: I can read minds. You must have suspected that I could because you have been keeping your mind blank of any thoughts except for the one that you had the moment you walked into the room this morning. Would you like to take a stab at what that thought was?"

"No, Ma'am, why don't you tell me what it was."

"Gladly," responded Ms. Leadbetter. "I believe your exact words were 'dang, I have a throbbing headache.'"

Instantly, David stood and darted to the door. He flung it open and zipped into the hallway. A few seconds later he backed his way into the room. Pushing him the whole way was Officer Halfpenny, happy to be doing his job.

"No . . . you have to tell me how to make them stop," pleaded David. "I can do this. I know I can."

Officer Halfpenny looked over at Ms. Leadbetter and waited for her directions.

She nodded. "He's dead to me. Take him away." She flung the back of her hand through the air as if to dismiss both of them at the same time.

"No!" yelled David. He ran back to his desk and grabbed the pencil that was sitting there. "I can make this stupid thing move. Just watch me." He reached way back and then launched the pencil directly at Ms. Leadbetter. His aim was true. Like a guided missile, it soared through the air honing in on its target: Ms. Leadbetter's left eye.

Ms. Leadbetter's eyes bulged just before her eye brows curved into deep dark frowns. How dare one of her students think he could hurl a pencil at her! She held up one hand like a police officer trying to stop a car. The pencil stopped about a foot in front of her hand and waited for instructions. Without hesitating, she flicked her index finger against her thumb, and the pencil reversed its course, tumbling through the air back at David.

David held his arms in front of his face for protection, which he needed. The pencil struck one of his arms and fell to the floor. Luckily it had never been sharpened, or it probably would have stuck in his arm like a dart.

"Why are you still here?" asked Ms. Leadbetter with an irritated voice.

"Sorry, Ma'am," replied Officer Halfpenny, "I jus never seen anythin like that befo."

"Yes, neither have I," said Ms. Leadbetter. "I've never been attacked by one of my students *before*." She said the word 'before' in such a way that made it seem like she was teaching the officer how to speak correctly.

"I wasn't talking 'bout the student; I meant you."

Ms. Leadbetter rolled her eyes. "I knew exactly what your thought was before it ever rolled out of your illiterate mouth."

"My what?" Officer Halfpenny was getting offended.

"Just do your job. Take this boy and get him processed like the others."

Halfpenny grabbed David's arm and led him out of the room.

"Ahh, ahh, Mr. Halfpenny," warned Ms. Leadbetter, "watch those nasty thoughts of violence, especially toward me. I might just have to do something about them."

He shook his head while he escorted David to the hallway and closed the door behind them.

Ms. Leadbetter slammed a hand down on top of a desktop and said, "Well, it's been an exciting morning, and we haven't even begun our lesson yet. Can we please get started, or do any of the four of you have any other questions?"

Well, she did ask, thought Bridgette, *even if it did sound a bit rhetorical.*

Bridgette raised a timid hand in the air.

Ms. Leadbetter reared back as if she couldn't believe what she was seeing. "Are you serious, Bridgette?"

Serious as a heart attack, she thought.

"What does it mean to be processed?"

"I ask the questions around here," Ms. Leadbetter replied. "My job is to ask, and your job is to answer. Is that clear?"

Bridgette sat there in utter silence.

"Because if it's not clear, we can make a phone call home and cancel this class for you. Of course, that would cancel your scholarship, your home, your parents' jobs, and yada, yada, yada. Do you understand?"

Bridgette nodded.

"There, you see. That wasn't too difficult, was it? I asked, you answered. Life as we know it is back to normal again.

"Now that we remember who is in control, let's get started. Bridgette and George, sit in the very back of the room. I want both of you to take turns trying to lift each other off your seats, using just your thoughts." She turned to the other two students, Tom and Cassandra. "As for you two, your time is running out, and my patience is wearing thin." She walked closer to them and put her wicked face right in their line of sight. "Move those pencils, or I'll get you before the headaches do."

Chapter 25

"You're hurting my arm," complained David.

Officer Halfpenny released his tight grip and said, "Don't you go tryin' any funny stuff." He patted his gun holster at his side. "I got jus the thing fer ya if ya do."

"You'd shoot me?" asked David.

"It's a taser, boy. Don'tcha know nothin'?"

They ambled to the end of the hallway and turned left where they walked down yet another hall until they reached the security office door. Through the door was a reception area with black vinyl chairs for visitors to use while they waited. A middle-aged woman in a baby blue security shirt stood behind a thick window that had a hole in it so that she could hear and be heard.

"Let us in, Marcy," called Officer Halfpenny.

The woman pushed a button, and a buzzer sounded off, which allowed Halfpenny to gain access to the large room Marcy worked in. He opened the door and led David to the tail end of the room. Way in the back sat two black metal jail cells, each large enough to fit a bed and a few feet of walking space – about twenty feet by twenty feet in area.

Halfpenny fished the keys from his pocket and unlocked one of the gates lined with iron bars. He swung it open and shoved David inside. "Git in there, boy."

"My name is David!" he yelled.

"Not anymore, it isn't."

"What's that supposed to mean?" David asked.

"You'll see soon enough. Believe it or not, you in there fer your own protection, ours too.

"Oh, and don't ask for any aspirin for those headaches you gittin' cuz it don't work. You bouts to go berserk in there."

"What?" said David. "You think locking me up is going to make me crazy?"

"Didn't say that," replied Halfpenny. "Said you was gonna go berserk."

"Do you mind elaborating a bit?" asked David. "I don't speak imbecile."

Halfpenny pointed at David through the bars. "Ya see there? You rich kids think ya got somethin' over on me, throwin' around them there fancy words jus like yer daddies throwin' around they money. But look at the pickle you in. Boy, I wouldn't give an ounce of spit to be in yer shoes right now."

David looked down at his shoes as if Halfpenny meant what he said literally.

"I'll tell you what's gonna happen to ya if ya tell me what ole Leadbetter's teachin' ya in that there classroom."

"She's not really teaching us anything," replied David. "She just makes us stare at pencils all day while trying to make them move with our minds."

"And you believe this nonsense?"

"Well, *I* can't do it," responded David, "but some of the others can."

"Is that right?" said Halfpenny while rubbing his chin. "I wonder why they would try to teach such a thing."

David suddenly grabbed his head with both hands. "Ahhh, I've gotta sit down. I have a splitting headache. This one is the worst yet." He sat on the bed that was merely a naked mattress with no sheets. He lay down on his back, eyes fixed on the ceiling while pounding his fists onto the mattress. "Make it stop! I can't take it!"

"Here we go again," said Halfpenny, more to himself than to David.

David leaped out of his bed like a spry cat. He clenched onto the bars and screamed.

Halfpenny took a few steps backward, though he knew from past experience that David would not be able to break out of the cell. He unsnapped the holster to his taser.

With severe tremors throughout his whole body, David yanked on the bars that imprisoned him. Then he let loose and started running the perimeter of the cell. It was like he was trying to build up speed. After two complete laps, he rammed into the unyielding metal bars with his shoulder. The force was so strong, it knocked him out. At least the pain was gone now.

Halfpenny holstered his taser and shook his head. "There goes another one." He pulled out his phone and made a call. "Hey, Charlie, we gots us another one. Pull the car around back tonight about tin o'clock so we can make the drop. Yeah, same deal as last time: a hunded bucks."

Halfpenny unlocked the cell and picked David from the ground and lay his limp body on the bed. He placed his arms behind his back and handcuffed them for safety.

***

The bell rang, and Ms. Leadbetter's class started to leave. Tom and Cassandra walked to the door and waited for their evil instructor to let them out. She stared down at them, and while opening the door, she said, "Tick tock." They scurried down the hallway.

George and Bridgette were last to leave.

"I saw you both back there lifting each other," said Ms. Leadbetter. "I think we can move to phase two in your training. From now on I want you to meet me in room 333 at 1:00."

"But what about Tom and Cassandra?" asked Bridgette.

Ms. Leadbetter's eyebrows shot upward. "Bridgette, darling, did you not learn anything in class today?"

George gave her a slight push in the back to remind her as well.

"Uh, sorry," she replied. "You ask the questions, and I give the answers."

"You're learning . . . slowly . . . but you're learning."

It felt almost like a compliment to Bridgette but not quite.

They left the classroom and walked toward the cafeteria.

"We should give Janice a call," said Bridgette.

George pulled his phone from his pants pocket and dialed Janice's number.

"Oooh, George, you got Janice's phone number?" teased Bridgette.

"Shut up; it's not what you think," said George defensively.

Suddenly, George put up a finger and said, "Hello . . . Janice, is that you? . . . Hello?" He gave Bridgette a worried look. "Somebody answered the phone, but no one's talking."

"We've gotta get over there," said Bridgette. She turned and started speed-walking toward the exit. George put his phone back in his pocket and trotted after her.

Within fifteen minutes they were outside Janice's bedroom window.

"She sleeps in there," said George.

They both put their faces to the window and tried to peek through the transparent white curtains.

"I think I see her," cried Bridgette.

"Where?" asked George.

"She's lying on her bed. It looks like she's sleeping or . . ."

Bang! Bang! Bang! George pounded on the window with his fist.

"She just lifted her head," said Bridgette in relief.

George's heart stopped thumping and began to relax again.

"Here she comes," said Bridgette.

The curtain pulled back, and the window slid open.

"What are you two doing here?" asked Janice in a groggy voice.

"You had us worried," said Bridgette. "The students in Leadbottom's class have almost all dropped out and become Berserkers. How's your head?"

"I don't know," responded Janice. "I slept in this morning. I was up all night reading the Bible. That Jesus dude is cool, and you're right. He makes a lot of sense."

"Well, we're glad to see you're okay," said Bridgette.

"Yeah," agreed George.

Janice looked behind her two friends with wide-open eyes. "Shoot! I think I see my dad coming home for lunch."

"What's wrong with that?" asked Bridgette.

"Uh, I'm supposed to be at school."

Maybe I'll tell you the real reason some other time.

Bridgette was able to read her mind.

"Quick!" Janice urged, "You have to get out of here before he sees you."

George and Bridgette ducked behind some bushes near the driveway where they waited to catch a glimpse of Janice's father.

A brown sedan pulled up. A tall middle-aged man with short dark hair and a mustache got out of the car. He wore a pair of black slacks and nice shoes, but it was difficult to see his shirt behind the long white lab coat that was draped around him. Through the tiny openings in the leaves of the bushes, Bridgette noticed a rectangular name tag on the coat. She couldn't read it, but she recognized the giant letters on it: LVSE, which stood for Las Vegas School of Excellence.

When the man entered the house, Bridgette said, "He works at our school."

"What?" said George, not trusting his own ears.

"She never told us that," said Bridgette.

"We never asked."

"He's wearing a lab coat," Bridgette pointed out. "He could have something to do with the experimental drugs they're using on us."

Their conversation was interrupted by Janice's dad yelling furiously. They couldn't make out what he was saying, but it was clear that he was not happy.

"Somebody's grumpy," said Bridgette.

"Ya think?" said George.

Bridgette's face turned serious. "Text Janice. Tell her to meet us at my house as soon as she can get away."

George quickly typed in the message. "Done."

Seconds later came the response. *Who is this?*

They heard the front door to the house click open.

"Run!" yelled Bridgette.

Chapter 26

After running in and out of several different alleys for about 15 minutes, Bridgette and George finally felt it was safe to walk. Little did they know they had run from one problem, only to step right into another.

They were breathing hard from all the running while walking cautiously down an alley in the middle of an unfamiliar neighborhood. The sun was beginning to set so it was getting dark in the shadowy shade shielded from the sun by the tall two-story houses.

George noticed the smoke first. "Uh oh, is that smoke I see ahead of us?"

Bridgette shifted her head left and then right. "Where are we anyway?"

"Looks like we've stumbled into Berserker territory," replied George. "Look, there are a couple of berserkers ahead of us."

"We'd better get out of this alley," suggested Bridgette. "It's not safe, especially after it gets completely dark."

"You read my mind," said George.

"Well, actually, I didn't," said Bridgette.

"I know; it was a figure of speech."

They both spun around while half-heartedly laughing at their confusion. When they did, the Alpha, dressed in his usual dirty white t-shirt, and six other berserkers were standing about 20 feet behind them. With his arms folded, the Alpha stood there, watching Bridgette's and George's smiles fade from their faces. The other berserkers stood by his side, hunched over with their arms hanging down.

"Run!" screamed George. He spun around and darted back toward the smoke at the other end of the alley.

"George!" yelled Bridgette. "Wait!"

George instantly switched out of fight or flight mode and slowed to a stop. He turned around and said, "I don't think the Alpha likes me."

"You've got to gain some courage, George," said Bridgette. "Like a lion."

Bridgette stared at the Alpha. "The Alpha can be quite unpredictable, but he seems to *think* more than the others. Just look at him with his arms folded while the others just let their arms hang like that. He has *body language*."

"Well, what's his body saying?" asked George, getting more nervous by the second.

"It almost looks like a stance of arrogance," said Bridgette.

"Try reading his mind?" suggested George.

"I'm trying, but he's not letting me in."

"I thought you didn't need permission," said George. He was getting fidgety.

"Normally, I don't. Maybe he's just not thinking about anything."

"Then why are they walking toward us?" said George with a scared voice.

"Wait! I think I'm getting something," said Bridgette.

George was preparing to start running again.

"Fire," said Bridgette.

"Fire?" repeated George. "What are we gonna do? They're getting closer?"

The Berserkers rushed forward with their arms stretched outward. George and Bridgette backpedaled and then scrambled toward the smoke, which was coming from a burning barrel.

After a few frantic footsteps, they discovered they were running into a trap. They were running toward more Berserkers than what they were running *away* from. The only thing they had going for them was that they hadn't been noticed by any of the others yet, but that would soon change.

The two kids trampled through a mixture of dirt and gravel between partial tall fences and the backs of buildings that formed the alley. Once they had been chased to the barrel, several adjacent berserkers looked up with their bloodshot eyes, attracted by the sudden movement. Slowly, they crept toward the intruders in their alley.

George and Bridgette both turned around to witness the Alpha and his six teenaged Berserkers heading toward them.

"What do we do?" asked George nervously.

"Let's see what they want," suggested Bridgette. "It's not like they're zombies and want to eat us."

The Alpha stepped up to Bridgette and clutched her arm with one of his large hands.

"Ow! That hurts!"

He yanked her forcefully toward the burning barrel.

Bridgette knew now what he was up to: revenge.

Just as he was about to thrust her arm over the flickering flames inside the barrel, Bridgette focused on making her body float upward. The Alpha's red eyes lit up, and he released her arm. All of the Berserkers, including George, raised their heads to watch Bridgette hover about 10 feet off the ground.

Bridgette gazed down at the Alpha and read his mind. He wasn't looking for revenge after all. He wanted a confirmation about the dream the other night. He was testing her.

So it's true, thought the Alpha.

"Of course, it's true," said Bridgette.

The Alpha lifted his hand high in the air and let out a barbaric yell. In response the rest of the Berserkers began walking away.

"How are you able to do that?" asked Bridgette.

I just can, thought the Alpha.

"Is he going to let us go?" asked George.

You can leave, but don't forget your promise.

"I won't," said Bridgette, "and perhaps we could even help each other."

I am of no use to anyone in this state, thought the Alpha.

"That's not true," responded Bridgette. "We all have value as human beings."

I'm not sure we qualify as human beings anymore.

"You are more valuable than you think," said Bridgette.'

"Uh, I hate to break up this bonding moment," interrupted George, "but we need to get home."

Bridgette dropped slowly back to the ground. While standing on her feet again, she said, "We have to go now, but I'll visit you tonight in your dreams to finish the conversation."

No fire this time, thought the Alpha. He grabbed his hand like it was still aching.

Bridgette smiled. "Of course not. Hey, you know what? You're a pretty nice guy. I wonder why the experiment didn't work on you."

The Alpha did not respond. He only moved aside and motioned for the rest of the Berserkers to make a path for them to pass.

Chapter 27

Three Years ago

Alan Cooper, Janice's dad, was relaxing comfortably in his white lab coat at his desk in his office. His feet were resting on his desk while he spoke on the phone. "That's right, the rats are all performing better than expected. I'm tempted to inject myself with the stuff. Well, yes, I'm *that* confident it will work. Uh, Ms. Leadbetter, I realize you're in a hurry, but shouldn't we try it on chimps first?" Very well, we can start tomorrow. Bring him to the lab at 8:00 in the morning."

Thirty minutes later across town Ms. Leadbetter paid a visit to a local orphanage.

"Come in, come in," said the case manager. "Please have a seat." Her dark hair was twirled and pinned on her head.

Ms. Leadbetter, dressed in a gray business suit, stepped into the lady's office and sat in the chair across from her desk.

The lady walked back to her desk and sat down as well. "I'm Mrs. Olson, the case manager here." She extended her arm to shake hands.

Ms. Leadbetter refused and said, "Oh, I'm getting over a cold so I'd better not."

"Yes, well, what can I do for you, Ms. ......?"

"Leadbetter. I'm looking for a young man, perhaps around 12 years old."

"I see," replied Ms. Olson. "Does this boy have a name?"

"I don't think I'm making myself clear," said Ms. Leadbetter. "I would like to know if you have any 12-year-old boys here in this facility."

Mrs. Olson slid her chair up to her computer. "Let me check." She typed a few buttons and then said, "Yes, we have one boy named Oscar. His parents died in a car crash about six months ago, and he has no other family, which is why he is here."

"Perfect, I'll take him, replied Ms. Leadbetter.

Mrs. Olson looked concerned. "Don't you want to meet him first before we begin filling out the custody papers?"

"Custody?" repeated Ms. Leadbetter. "Heavens, no. I'm not looking to adopt the boy.....just *borrow* him for a few days."

Mrs. Olson lifted her hand to her mouth and gasped at the thought. "Surely, you're joking with me. *"*

Ms. Leadbetter stared at the woman and read her mind. *What's in it for me?* thought Mrs. Olson.

"I assure you this is no joke," responded Ms. Leadbetter. She began rummaging in her purse.

Mrs. Olson stood from her chair and said, "Well, I think we're done here. We do not rent our children out. This is a legitimate orphanage. Now, if you......"

Ms. Leadbetter plopped five one hundred dollar bills on the table. "I'm willing to pay you for your trouble. No harm will come to the boy."

Mrs. Olson's eyes lit up. *I could use the money to pay my dentist bill.*

"I love your smile, by the way," said Ms. Leadbetter. "You must have a wonderful dentist."

"Well, thank you," replied Ms. Olson. She walked over to her office door and closed it quietly. She walked back to her chair, sat down, and said with a lowered voice, "How long would he be gone.....you know, in case his social worker wants to meet with him?"

Ms. Leadbetter's lips curled upward. "Oh, I'd say just a couple of days."

When Mrs. Olson reached for the money, Ms. Leadbetter placed her hand over it and said, "So, do we have a deal?"

"No one can know," said Mrs. Olson.

"Perfect," agreed Ms. Leadbetter. She lifted her hand and freed the money.

Mrs. Olson folded the money and placed it in her purse. "I'll see to him personally. This way I will be the only one who knows of his whereabouts."

"Splendid," said Ms. Leadbetter. "I'll go pull my car up front."

"You mean you want him right now?"

"Time is money," responded Ms. Leadbetter. "You have your money; I would like what I paid for."

Mrs. Olson's conscience was bothering her. "What did you say you needed him for?"

"I didn't." Ms. Leadbetter picked a card from her jacket with two fingers and flicked it, making a popping noise. "Here's my card in case you need to contact me."

That seemed to make Mrs. Olson calm down a bit and more agreeable.

"I'll go get him."

"I'll be waiting in my car out front," said Ms. Leadbetter.

Moments later Mrs. Olson brought Oscar to Ms. Leadbetter's car. She opened his door and closed it for him once he climbed inside. She looked around suspiciously and then scampered back into the building.

Ms. Leadbetter turned and looked at the boy. "So you're Oscar?"

"Yes, ma'am."

Oscar's dark hair was clean cut around his ears. He had bangs down to his eyebrows. His arms were thin but muscular for his age.

"Well, you look like a strong young man. Are you in good shape?"

"I do 100 push ups and 100 sit ups every day," he replied with a smile.

"Impressive," said Ms. Leadbetter.

"So, are you looking to adopt?" asked Oscar. "I'm a really good kid. I'm no trouble at all. I'm only here because my parents died."

"Let's just take this one day at a time," replied Ms. Leadbetter. "I'm going to introduce you to a man named Alan. He works for me. You'll be helping him with his work. If this goes well, we can talk more about all of that.....uh....complicated stuff."

"I can do that," beamed Oscar.

I'm going to do such a good job, she's going to want to adopt me on the spot, he thought.

Ms. Leadbetter obviously read his thoughts and smiled. "I think we're going to have a wonderful relationship."

Oscar clapped his hands together. "I can't wait to get started."

Ms. Leadbetter and Oscar pulled up to a large warehouse facility, an extension of the Las Vegas School of Excellence.

"Where are we?" asked Oscar.

"This is Dr. Alan Cooper's laboratory. He's a good scientist. A bit cocky at times, but nonetheless, he's pretty good at what he does. Just don't tell him I told you so."

I wonder how I'm going to be able to help him, thought Oscar.

"Now, remember, you do a good job here with Dr. Cooper, and we'll look more into all of that adoption stuff. Do exactly as he says. I'll pick you up later this evening."

"Yes, ma'am."

Ms. Leadbetter escorted Oscar into the lab.

Alan met them at the door as soon as they entered. "Well, this must be the young man that's come to help us with our research." He held out his hand.

Oscar shook his hand and said, "Pleased to meet you. I'm a quick learner, and I'll do my best."

"I'm sure you'll do you just fine."

"Well, I'll leave you two to your business," said Ms. Leadbetter. "See you around dinner time." She handed a vial of blood to Alan. "Here, I hope it's the last vial of my blood you'll need." She turned and walked away.

He slipped it into his lab coat and said, "Sorry, but you're our only source." He looked down at Oscar. "Come on, Oscar, let me show you around. I've got some rats I want you to meet."

"Cool."

"Oh, they're more than cool," responded Dr. Cooper. "They can do some pretty neat tricks."

"Like what?"

"I'll let you see for yourself." He led Oscar down a small hallway and then opened up a door that revealed the large open-spaced warehouse.

Oscar's jaw dropped open when he saw what was inside. There were hundreds of long rectangular tables standing everywhere. Some tables held cages while others had lots and lots of test tubes and beakers filled with all kinds of colorful liquids.

Dr. Cooper led Oscar to the first group of small animal cages made from gray wire. He opened up a cage and pulled out a white albino rat with red eyes. "Let's show you what Alpha-47 can do."

They walked a few tables down that were waist high until they came to a transparent glass cage that was almost as big as the table itself, about four feet wide and 10 feet long. There was a gigantic maze on the bottom of the cage, but the upper half had nothing but space. The cage was about three feet tall.

Dr. Cooper opened a small door to the cage and placed the rat at the beginning of the maze. Under the table was a mini refrigerator where the scientist reached inside and grabbed a chunk of cheese. He then opened another small door on the other side and dropped the cheese at the end of the maze.

"Okay, now let's see what trick Alpha-47 has up his sleeve," said Dr. Cooper.

Oscar's eyes were glued on the rat. Alpha-47 lifted its nose and started sniffing the air. He began walking the maze until he came to his first dead end. Instead of just turning around to find another route, he did something that opened Oscar's eyes wide. All four feet slowly lifted upward. When he was high above the maze, he pedaled his little feet, swatting at the air. Slowly, he moved forward toward the end of the maze bypassing all the turns and dead ends. Once he saw the cheese, he lowered himself down until his feet touched the bottom next to his reward. He picked up the cheese with his little paws and began nibbling on it.

"I don't believe it," said Oscar. "A rat that can fly."

"That's not all," said Dr. Cooper.

"What else can he do?" asked Oscar anxiously.

"When he's hungry enough, I can place a piece of cheese on the table outside his wire cage while he's inside. He will bite the wires on the cage to try and get out until he gets too frustrated. Then he stops and stares at it. After a few seconds the cheese begins to slide across the table toward the cage until he can grab it through the wires."

"Amazing!"

"These are some exciting times," said Dr. Cooper.

"So what do you want me to do to help?" asked Oscar. "Do you want me to feed the rats? Clean the cages?"

"Didn't Ms. Leadbetter explain to you why you're here?"

"I thought it was to be your assistant," replied Oscar.

Dr. Cooper scratched his chin. "Well, you will be assisting me; that's true, but what I *really* need you to do is to be Alpha-48."

"Alpha-48," repeated Oscar. He thought for a moment and then said, "Oh, you want to use me as your next experiment. Is it safe?"

"All my Alpha-40s rats are still alive and kicking."

"What about the 30s and 20s?" asked Oscar with a worried tone.

"Well, that was when I was in the early stages of perfecting the serum. Some of them are still alive, but that was an entirely different strain of the formula from what I'm using now."

"I don't know," said Oscar. "It sounds kind of risky."

"Don't you want to be able to fly and move things with your mind?"

"Yeah, but I could die," replied Oscar.

"Well, Ms. Leadbetter could always take you back. I'll give her a call, and she can come and pick you up." He reached for his cell phone from his pocket.

"Wait! Okay, I'll do it," said Oscar glumly.

"That's the spirit. I don't think you realize yet just how lucky you are to be in this situation."

"Can I still take care of the rats?"

"Of course," agreed Dr. Cooper. "You'll need to keep yourself busy so you don't get bored while we make our observations."

"When do we get started?"

Dr. Cooper lifted a syringe from his pocket and pulled off the protective covering from the tip of the needle. "No sense in waiting. I've waited long enough to move forward with this."

For the first couple of days Oscar fed the rats in their cages. Alpha-27 had lost all of its hair and looked very weak. Alpha-35's behavior was very aggressive. Oscar knew he would bite his finger if he put it through the metal wires. Alpha-43 kept slamming his head into the walls of his cage. This had Oscar worried because 43 is not that far away from 48, which was his number.

"I'm worried about Alpha-43," said Oscar to Dr. Cooper in his office. "He keeps ramming his head into wall. I think he's going to kill himself."

"He's just a rat, Oscar," said Dr. Cooper.

"I'm not worried for the rat. I'm worried for myself."

"Oh, I see what you mean," said Dr. Cooper. "Well, I wouldn't get too bent out of shape. The only rat you should concern yourself with is Alpha-47. He's the one with the same serum as you.

"How are you feeling today anyway?"

"Fine."

"Are you writing in that journal I gave you? Remember, I want you to write down how you're feeling and also anything that happens that's unusual."

"Yep."

"Good boy." Dr. Cooper messed up Oscar's hair with his hand.

On the third day of the experiment Oscar wrote down the usual comments in his journal about no new changes or feelings. In frustration he slammed his pencil on the table next to his journal and stared at it. He squinted his eyes, and it began to roll across the table top. His eyes bulged open.

"It moved!" He scrambled across the warehouse floor up to Dr. Cooper's office. "Dr. Cooper! Dr. Cooper!"

Dr. Cooper looked up from his desk. "What is it? What's wrong?"

"It moved! It moved!"

"Slow down, Alpha-48…..I mean Oscar. What moved?"

"My pencil! I made it move with my mind!"

Dr. Cooper stood from his chair excitedly. "Show me." He pulled a pen from his pocket and placed it on his desk.

Oscar concentrated on it. It moved slightly but not as much as the pencil because the pen wouldn't roll due to the clip that prevented it from doing so.

"This is the breakthrough we've been waiting for!" exclaimed Dr. Cooper.

Oscar smiled. "So we're done? Ms. Leadbetter's gonna adopt me now?"

"Sorry, 48, the experiment has just begun. Now we need to be even more detailed with our observations. Even the slightest changes need to be noted. You might even be able to fly one day."

A couple of weeks later Oscar was doing his daily rounds of feeding the rats when he noticed Alpha-47 squealing in agony. He would look fine one moment, and the next he'd be crying and lying on his side.

Dr. Cooper put his hand on Oscar's shoulder. "Don't think too much into it, 48. He's just a rat. The human body systems are far superior to those of a rat. What you see here does not mean the same thing will happen to you. After all, you haven't learned to fly yet, and he can."

It was about this time that Oscar began to change. He was withdrawn and seemed to lose his happy-go-lucky attitude. He stopped speaking, even to Dr. Cooper, who was beginning to lose his patience with his test subject, especially since communication was vital for his experiment.

Twenty days after the experiment began Oscar experienced his first headache. He was lying in bed at Ms. Leadbetter's house. Through the pain all he could think about was Alpha-47 lying on his side squealing while he did the same. He screamed in agony, curled into a fetal position. It only lasted a minute or two, but it felt like an hour.

Ms. Leadbetter rushed into the room after reading his mind and said, "You're *still* going to the lab tomorrow."

He gazed up at her. His eyes were bloodshot with zigzags of blood vessels running through them.

She reared back and said, "And get some sleep. You look like you haven't slept in days."

He was in too much pain to think bad thoughts about her. Convinced she wouldn't read his mind of any foul thoughts about her, she left the room, not suspecting what he would do the following day.

When he arrived at the lab the next morning, Dr. Cooper said, "Ms. Leadbetter told me you had a bad headache last night, 48. Don't forget to write that down in your journal. And write down those bloodshot eyes too. Didn't you get any sleep last night?"

Oscar nodded, grabbed the rat food, and walked into the warehouse while Dr. Cooper stared at his computer in his office. Oscar picked up his journal from a nearby table and began to write in it. He pressed down so hard the tip of his pencil broke. Reaching back as if the journal were a flying disc, he flung it across the room. It flapped a couple of times like a small bird before it cartwheeled on the ground and came to a halt. The last words he had written were exposed and staring out of the book: *I'm nobody's guinea pig.* That would be his last journal entry. He looked back at the office door. Dr. Cooper was still working. Cautiously, he pushed the side door open and stepped outside into a new chapter of his life.

Nobody reported his disappearance, and Mrs. Olson finally stopped calling Ms. Leadbetter when she realized there was nothing she could do. If she reported the missing boy, she would get into big trouble. Instead, she hid his paperwork, and the search for Oscar, Alpha-48, ended before it even began.

Chapter 28

That night at dinner Bridgette could hear the thoughts of her family members. Her mom was hoping that everyone liked what she cooked; her dad was wondering if he'd get to watch the second half of the football game after dinner, and her little brother, Tommy, was wondering how he could hide the green food on his plate so he wouldn't have to eat it.

Bridgette stared at Tommy's broccoli until it floated above his plate. A smile spread across Tommy's face. He knew what was going on. He opened his mouth wide and allowed Bridgette to feed him from across the table.

Their mom noticed Tommy eating and said, "That's a good boy. Eating all your vegetables so you can grow up big and strong."

She looked across the table at Bridgette. "How was school today, dear? Anything unusual?"

Bridgette thought for a moment and then said, "George and I are going to start meeting with Ms. Leadbetter in room 333 starting tomorrow. That's where we're going to continue our training."

"Sounds like you two are progressing nicely."

"Yeah, we're the only ones," Bridgette pointed out.

"What about Janice?" asked her mom.

"I'm worried about her. She was supposed to come over today after school, but she never came."

"I'm sure she'll tell you what happened tomorrow at school."

"I don't know, Mom," said Bridgette. "I have a feeling if I don't see her tonight, I may never see her again."

"What are you talking about?" her mom asked. "What else is going on that you're not telling me?"

"It's too much to explain and not enough time to do it."

Her mom looked at her dad. "Honey, can you drive Bridgette over to Janice's house after dinner?"

Bridgette's father turned his head from the football game and said, "Huh?"

"Bridgette needs a ride to her friend's house."

"Sure," he replied, "right after the game."

"Never mind, I'll do it," said her mom with an irritated tone.

"Thanks, Mom," said Bridgette. "Your perfume smells nice, by the way."

"Thanks, it's new." She pulled the bottle from her purse and handed it to her daughter.

Bridgette sprayed a sample on her wrist and rubbed her wrists together and then smelled it. She nodded. "Nice."

Her mom sighed. "Well, let's get going before it gets any later."

***

At eight o'clock sharp Charlie knocked on the back door next to the jail cell. Halfpenny opened the door, and they both helped carry David to the squad car.

They drove around for a while to make sure they weren't being followed. When they felt safe enough to do it, the security officers pulled over next to an alley of Berserkers and threw David's body on the ground.

"That makes the seventh one in the past two months," said Charlie.

"Das seven hunded bucks fo you and me," replied Halfpenny.

"Man, why do you always have to sound like you got your education watching gangster rap music videos?" asked Charlie.

"You jus jealous," replied Officer Halfpenny.

"You sound ridiculous," said Charlie. "I know you didn't sound this way during your interview."

"Jus lemme be. Dis is how I roll."

Charlie shook his head. "Hey, don't forget to get your cuffs back," said Charlie. "Don't wanna leave around any evidence."

"Ain't dat the truth."

Halfpenny reached down with his key and unlatched the handcuffs from David's wrists.

"You sure he's gonna be okay just lying here by himself?" asked Charlie.

Officer Halfpenny put his cuffs in his pocket. He looked down the dark alley. "Those freaks'll find him; they always do."

***

Bridgette and her mom drove down the darkened streets toward Janice's house. They neared the pitch black alley, and Bridgette tried to look toward the fiery barrel she knew was there . . . burning and telling everyone that the Berserkers were in the area . . . and to stay away.

Just as they passed, Bridgette saw movement on the ground next to the sidewalk. "Mom! Wait!"

Her mother slowed until she came to a stop.

Bridgette rolled down the window, stuck out her head and looked behind them. "Go back, please."

The car rolled backwards and stopped next to the alley. Somebody was lying on the ground, trying to sit up.

Bridgette looked at the person. "Are you okay? Do you need any help?" She used the flashlight on her phone to shine at him. The light struck his eyes, which were all white with red crooked red lines running through them. It was David. He lifted his hand to keep the light away from his face.

"Go, Mom! Go!" yelled Bridgette. She hit the dashboard with her fist.

Mrs. Swanson jammed her foot on the gas pedal. The wheels squealed, and they sped up quickly down the street.

"Who was that?" asked Bridgette's mom.

"That was David . . . well, sort of."

"Sort of?"

"Yeah," replied Bridgette, "it used to be David, but now he's a Berserker. I suppose he's technically still David, but he's a Berserker now so he acts differently."

"A Berserker?"

142

"Yes, responded Bridgette, "that's what happens to the students who can't move their pencils."

"What happens?"

"They lose their minds," said Bridgette.

"Oh, my," said Mrs. Swanson. "Is this what's happening to Janice?"

"Not sure, Mom, but that's why we're headed over there. We need to see if Janice is okay."

Bridgette's mom looked worried. She turned to her and said, "Are you going to turn into a Berserker?"

"Of course not, Mom. The serum worked on me, remember?"

Mrs. Swanson shook her head. "I can't believe we let you go through with this. We knew they were doing some sort of experiment, but we didn't think it could be harmful."

"It's not your fault, Mom," said Bridgette. "You didn't know that Ms. Leadbetter was this wicked."

A tear trickled down her mom's cheek. "But they paid for our house; they got us our jobs. We didn't just do what was best for you; we did what was best for the family."

"And I wouldn't have had it any other way," said Bridgette. "So don't blame yourself. I did this, and now I'm going to fix it."

Bridgette's mom pulled over to the side of the road. She gazed worriedly into her daughter's eyes. "You're going to *what?*"

"We're working on a plan," replied Bridgette.

"Is it safe?"

"Um, safe is a relative term, Mom."

"Relative?"

"Well, yeah," said Bridgette, "I mean is it safer than playing with firecrackers? Probably not. Is it safer than playing with a stick of dynamite? Perhaps."

"Oh, Bridgette, what are you getting yourself into?"

"Don't worry, Mom. If it gets to be too dangerous, we'll terminate the plan."

"Be careful, dear; your safety is more important than any job or house."

"Don't worry, Mom," assured Bridgette. "We got this." She reached over and hugged her mother tightly before they continued on their way.

Minutes later, Bridgette said, "This is it. Pull over right here." She pointed at Janice's house.

"It's awfully dark," said her mom. "Don't they even turn on a porch light?"

"Her dad's car's not there, so that's good, I think."

"Why is that good?" asked her mother.

"Something Janice was thinking earlier today when I read her mind. I have a feeling her father and her have issues."

Bridgette climbed out of the car. "Stay here; I'll be right back."

She slinked over to the front door and rang the doorbell. No answer. She knocked. Still no answer. While walking to the side of the house, she looked at her mother and held up one finger. Bridgette smiled when she saw Janice's window had still been left open. She looked inside, but her bedroom was empty. Walking back to where her mom could see her, she beckoned for her to come and help her.

Bridgette's mother walked up to her through the darkness and said, "Isn't she home?"

"It doesn't look like it, but I was hoping you could lift me up to her bedroom window so I could climb into the house."

"What? Are you crazy? Are you trying to get arrested? Absolutely not! Now let's go home."

"Mom," pleaded Bridgette, "you didn't see her today like I did. When her dad came home, she was terrified. Something's not right."

Her mom sighed. "Well, if you truly think she's in danger, I guess we should at least look, but this is against the law, and we could get in big trouble."

They walked up to the window. They checked to see if anyone was watching. It didn't appear that anyone was so Bridgette's mom put two hands down toward one of Bridgette's feet. Bridgette stepped onto them. Lifting and grunting at the same time, Bridgette's mom hoisted her daughter up and through the window.

"I don't know why you didn't just use your new ability to do this," said her mom.

Bridgette stood there feeling silly. "You're right. I could have easily elevated my body up. I guess I'm just a bit nervous and scared for Janice. Would you like me to elevate you?"

She shook her head. "No, I'm not coming in. I'll wait out here in case her dad comes home in the car. Do you have your phone on you?"

"Yeah."

"Good, I'll text you if he shows up."

Her mom walked back to the car.

Bridgette whispered, "Janice." She didn't want to risk turning on any lights in fear that it would give her trespassing away.

With no lights on, the house was pitch black. She felt her way around the bedroom and then into the hallway where she slid her hands on the walls while she walked to help guide her to where she thought the living room would be. Halfway across the living room floor, she stepped and tripped on something. She went down with a thud. If anyone was home, she would surely be found out now.

She lay still on the wooden floor and listened intensely. No footsteps, nothing. Wait. There *was* something.

Help me.

The floor seemed to be talking to her.

Help me; I'm in the cellar.

Chapter 29

An eerie feeling had crept out of the darkness and grabbed hold of Bridgette. It felt like a ghost was speaking to her. For all she knew, it was exactly that. Her desperation to find Janice was the only thing that kept her shaky legs moving forward. Looking like a toddler, she crawled across the floor, slowly and gingerly, as the floorboards cracked and squealed beneath the weight of her slender frame.

I can hear you, said the voice.

Bridgette stopped crawling and waited.

Wait! Where'd you go? Lord, Jesus, please let it be Bridgette.

Bridgette began crawling again, faster this time.

Look inside the pantry. You'll find the trap door in the pantry.

Pantry, thought Bridgette. *Who has a pantry? What is a Pantry anyway?*

It had the word 'pan' in it, so Bridgette figured it had to be near the kitchen. Cautiously, she turned her cell phone flashlight on and kept it pointed at the ground so that she could see where she was going. She saw the white linoleum kitchen floor in front of her with a white door next to the stove.

When she reached the door, she stood and grabbed the small knob. *One…two…three.*

Deliberately, she slowly turned the knob and pulled on the door. It creaked open, and while it did, Bridgette squinted her eyes as if it were the sound fingernails made while scratching down a chalkboard. She pointed her flashlight at the floor inside the pantry, lighting up the metal trap door that was shut and locked with a screwdriver. It really wasn't locked; the screwdriver had merely been thrust through the latch so that the door could not be opened from below. *One…two…three.*

She kneeled down and grabbed the screwdriver and withdrew it from the latch, allowing the door to be freely opened.

She waited and listened.

What are you waiting for? asked the ghostly voice.

What are you *waiting for?* wondered Bridgette.

After a moment of silence, Bridgette wrapped her fingers around the rusty metal handle and swung the door open, letting it rest softly on the floor inside the pantry. Dust had been stirred up, and she could see it drifting through the air within the beam of light emanating from her phone. She looked down into the black hole and shivered. Standing on wobbly legs, she shined her light on the steps going downward. There was a light switch next to the ladder.

Thank God, she thought.

She reached into the pit. The darkness swallowed her arm but would not taste more of her, not if she could help it. Blindly, her fingers searched for the switch. Finally, they found it and flipped it upward: Click! Instantly, the cellar flooded with light. She could see the floor at the bottom of the ladder but nothing else; the descent was too steep, and the walls blocked her field of vision.

She put her face into the hole and whispered softly, "Is anyone down there?"

No answer.

Bridgette felt faint and then inhaled deeply. She didn't realize she had been holding her breath. She turned around and started backing down the ladder one shaky foot and then one trembling leg at a time.

Halfway down the ladder, she was able to look across the cellar floor to the other side of the room. Sitting in a wooden chair with ropes wrapped around her legs and waist, Janice sat there twisting back and forth like she was trying to break free. Her mouth was taped so she could only make a low muffling sound.

Upon seeing this inhumane sight, Bridgette swallowed her fear of the unknown and quickly climbed down the ladder with an angry look on her face.

Halfway across the floor, it happened. Another vision began to take form.

Bridgette was sitting in a chair with a shiny silver helmet on her head. Wires protruding from the helmet were connected to a large metal box that looked to be some sort of power source. Colorful lights were blinking, lighting up her head like a Christmas tree. She had a blank stare on her face, and her eyes were dark.

Suddenly, Janice and George crash through a door and stumble into the room.

Once they notice Bridgette in the chair, Ms. Leadbetter steps out of hiding and says, "I knew you'd come for your pathetic friend." She turns around. "Release the planes!"

"Das what I'm talkin' 'bout," replied Officer Halfpenny. While punching a few buttons on his remote control box in his hand, he says, "Charlie, git yer plane off the ground."

Two planes, each about a foot in length, buzzed into action.

One plane locked onto George, but George bravely faced the plane while concentrating on throwing it off course. He swung his head to the side, and the plane zoomed toward the wall and exploded upon impact.

"Ha! You're gonna have to do better than these little toys," bragged George.

Right after the words left his mouth, another plane ambushed him from the side. It wasn't that close, and it didn't need to be. It fired a few strong bolts of electricity at George, which zapped him in the shirt. They sparked and smoked while George's body locked up and fell to the ground. He lay on the floor screaming, "I can't move!"

Ms. Leadbetter ran up to George. "Quick! "We need another helmet for this one."

Suddenly, a familiar sound snapped her out of the future. She looked down at her phone. It was a text from her mom.

HER DEAD IS HER

Bridgette shook her head to wake herself up. She read the text again and then typed a question mark and hit "send."

She ran across the floor and tore the tape from Janice's mouth.

"Thank you for rescuing me from this *dungeon*," said Janice. "You just had another vision of the future, didn't you?"

Bridgette nodded and started working on untying the knots on the rope when her phone beeped again. Another message from her mom.

HER DAD IS HERE!

STUPID AUTO CORRECT

"Your dad is here!" exclaimed Bridgette. "Why did he tie you up?" She finished untying her legs and continued working on the knots around the back of the chair.

"He thinks I'm going to turn into a Berserker," replied Janice.

"Well, are you?" said Bridgette frantically.

"Can a Berserker move a pencil with her mind?" asked Janice.

"No," answered Bridgette. She untied the last knot and pulled the ropes free from Janice's body.

"Then no," said Janice triumphantly. "I'm not going to turn into a Berserker."

"Thank God," said Bridgette. She reached over and hugged Janice.

Janice raised her arms to break up the embrace. "Whoa now, let's not get too touchy." She stood and darted toward the ladder. When she reached it, she climbed to the top and gingerly pulled the door shut, encasing them inside. She turned off the light and quietly descended back to the bottom.

"What should we do?" asked Bridgette, not knowing what Janice's dad was up to.

Janice sat back in the chair. "Quick, tie me back up."

Bridgette bent down and picked up the rope. "How does your dad know about Berserkers?"

"Because he helped create them," replied Janice.

"He what?"

"Well, it's not like he tried to; it was an accident. A small price to pay for science he claims."

"Does that include his own daughter?" said Bridgette rhetorically. She finished tying her last knot and started looking around for a hiding spot.

Chapter 30

Ten minutes after the sounds of clanging pots and pans, Janice's dad turned on the lights and stepped gingerly down the stairs. He was carrying a bowl of soup and a sandwich that had been cut in half, each piece sitting on a saucer, the same saucer the steaming bowl was on.

After reaching the bottom, he kicked a large empty box toward Janice. It bumped up against her legs and stopped. Carefully, he set the soup and sandwich on top of it. He reached for Janice's mouth to remove the tape and then realized it was gone.

"How'd you get the tape off?" he asked suspiciously.

Janice thought quickly. "I … uh … used my tongue and wiggled it off."

He looked on the floor. "Then where is it?"

"I ate it."

"You what?" he said shocked.

"It's not like you've given me anything to eat lately," complained Janice.

"That sounds like something a Berserker would do," suggested her father.

"Do I *look* like a Berserker?" asked Janice with an angry look.

"I'm still not taking any chances. I'll be back; I'm going to get you a spoon. I half-expected you to already be a Berserker, and we know they don't use spoons."

"Hurry, I'm starving." Janice picked up her sandwich and took a bite.

Bridgette waited until she could hear footsteps going up the staircase before she came out of hiding. She appeared from behind Janice. "I'm going to get you out of here."

"Let's just wait until he leaves," whispered Janice.

"Okay," agreed Bridgette. "I'll just hide back over here behind the water heater."

Janice's father came skipping down the stairs just as Bridgette hid herself again. Spoon in hand, he walked up to Janice and stopped. "What's that?"

"What's what?" asked Janice.

"That smell. It smells like perfume."

"Uh … I don't smell anything," lied Janice.

"Is there someone down here with you?"

"Yeah, Dad … a whole group of Berserkers. We're gonna take over the world."

He raised his head and sniffed. "No, it's not a Berserker. He lifted his nose and followed the scent toward the water heater.

Bridgette heard him and phoned her mother. Luckily, she answered right away. Just before Janice's father discovered her, Bridgette revealed herself, walking out calmly saying, "Hi, Mom, can you come downstairs at Janice's and get me?"

"What's wrong?" asked her mother.

"Thanks, Mom, I'll see you in a minute."

Janice's father snatched the phone from her and said, "What do you think you're doing down here?"

"I think the better question is 'what do you think you're doing, tying up your daughter?'"

"It's not the way it looks."

"You taped her mouth," responded Bridgette angrily.

He stepped toward Bridgette. "I can see you're not going to be reasonable about this. That's a pity."

Bridgette took a step backwards. Her heart thumped, and her legs trembled.

Her phone beeped because it received a message.

Janice's father read it. *Use your powers before I get there, if you have to.*

"Powers? You've got to be kidding me. What are you going to do … chase me with a floating pencil? I've heard about your minimal progress in Ms. Leadbetter's class."

His smugness only caused Bridgette to regain her courage and remember that she did have power, a lot more power than he knew.

Bridgette focused on the spoon still in Janice's father's hand. With her telekinesis she willed it to fly out of his hand and then thwack him on the head.

He reached up with a quick reflex and yelled, "Owwww!"

"How's that for a floating pencil?" asked Bridgette smartly.

He thought, *I'm going to have to tie this one up too. This is getting out of hand. I need to come up with a plan.*

"Did you not hear that my mom was on her way?" asked Bridgette. "You can't tie me up anyway. I won't let you."

Janice's father looked surprised. "You can-"

"Yes, I can read minds too. Didn't Ms. Leadbetter tell you that?"

As soon as the words rolled out of her lips, she realized Ms. Leadbetter did *not* know about her mindreading ability and would now, because of her big mouth, soon be told.

They were interrupted by a pounding on the front door. It echoed all the way down the stairs.

"My mom!" cried Bridgette. "We're getting out of here."

"My daughter stays. It's not safe out there for her or anyone near her."

Bridgette crinkled her eyebrows. "The only place that's not safe is here with you. What kind of parent ties up his own daughter?" She hurried over to Janice and began untying the rope from her friend.

"I told you to leave her alone." He lunged at the girls.

Bridgette held one hand out, and Janice's father rose slowly off the ground.

He kicked his legs frantically. "What the heck! Let me down this instant!"

"Don't hurt him," said Janice. "I mean, don't hurt him a lot."

Bridgette shook her head. "Are you kidding? I jumped over a cockroach when I first came down here. Even a cockroach has a right to live." She turned and looked up at Janice's dad floating in the air. "Even if the cockroach has two legs and squirms a lot."

"I like your feistiness," said Janice.

"Janice, don't leave!" pleaded her father. "You're going to turn into a monster. You're a danger to everyone, including yourself."

"Chill out, Dad. I've been trying to tell you; I'm not going to turn into a Berserker. Watch this."

She gazed down at the spoon that had fallen to the floor earlier. Slowly, it began floating upward. Then it dropped and clanged on the floor.

"Happy?" said Janice.

Janice's father's eyes began to glow. A relieved look came over his face, and a tear trickled down the side of one cheek. "But the headaches."

"All gone," explained Janice.

"But how-"

"Not *how*, Dad … *who*."

Her dad looked bewildered.

"Jesus. I've been saved, and I suggest you do the same while you still have time."

Between the pounding sounds on the door, they could hear Bridgette's mom screaming her name.

"Let's get out of here, Janice," urged Bridgette.

"But he'll come after us," said Janice.

"No, he won't," responded Bridgette. "He's not worried about you anymore. In fact, he's relieved. The only thing he's thinking about now is going back to the lab and creating another experimental serum based off of what he just learned here today."

"Oh, Dad, just quit," pleaded Janice. "Look what you're doing to people. Look what you did to Mom."

"That was her own choice, honey. Don't go blaming me for what she wanted. I've got to find a way to stop all these unwanted side effects. No more Berserkers."

"Don't you get it?" said Bridgette. "It's not the serum you need to change; it's the person." She pushed Janice toward the stairs.

Once Janice was safely up the stairs, Bridgette ran up the steps as well. Janice's father collapsed to the floor the moment she climbed out of the cellar.

The girls and Mrs. Swanson ran to the car, jumped inside, and drove away.

Chapter 31

Two years ago, approximately one year after Oscar's failed lab experiment, Janice and her parents were living a peaceful life in Las Vegas. Janice's father, Dr. Cooper, Dr. *Alan* Cooper, was a top researcher at the Las Vegas School of Excellence. He was on the verge of a breakthrough, so he thought. He was so excited and very confident in his findings. Each night he came home and told his family how close he was getting and how his research was going to make normal people amazing.

Janice's mother, Hilda, was sick and tired of being Mrs. Cooper, also known as Dr. Cooper's wife. It's not that she didn't love her husband, but she didn't feel like she had an identity of her own. It seemed no one ever called her Hilda. Even Janice called her Mom.

One day Mr. Cooper came home from work early, just after Janice returned to the house from her elementary school. He opened the door and lifted Janice high in the air and twirled her around. "I did it!" he exclaimed. "This gamma ray machine is changing everything."

Janice smiled while she hugged her father's neck and gazed into his eyes.

"Wow, you're getting to be too heavy to lift," he said. Slowly, he allowed her to plop to the floor. "Where's your mother?"

"Right behind you," replied Hilda. "Did you really do it?" Her eyes were opened wide, and a glum look stretched across her face.

Alan looked as if he might pop at any moment. All he could do was nod his head. "I can't wait for human trials! I think we've solved the headache problem too."

"Why wait?" asked Hilda.

"Because it's protocol," responded Alan. "They're not my rules; they're the rules of the organization, and they're there for everyone's safety. Don't forget what happened the last time we jumped the gun. That was a disaster."

Hilda walked up to her husband and stared him in the eyes. "Come on, honey, rules were made to be broken. Give it to me. Let me do this. No one has to know."

As tempting as it was, Mr. Cooper had to decline the offer. "Sorry, honey, I just can't take the chance. You have a daughter to consider."

"Janice wants me to do it too, don't you dear?"

Both parents gazed at their only daughter.

Janice looked uneasy for a moment, but she knew how to answer those kinds of questions, the kind that persuade you to agree. "Yes, if it will make you happy."

"But ... what if something goes wrong?" asked Janice's father with a concerned tone.

"Nothing will go wrong," replied Hilda. "You're a brilliant scientist, and you've been working on this for so long. Besides, I don't think I can go on living this way. I need some excitement in my life. It feels like this Las Vegas air has sucked the life right out of me."

Alan sighed. "All right, let's do it, but it has to be done in secret. No one is to know about this. I could lose my job if they find out. I'll bring home a syringe tomorrow to administer it." He kissed her on the forehead. "Get ready; your life is about to change."

"It's about time something is finally going to go right for me."

That night while Janice's dad tucked her in her bed, Janice said, "Dad, what's a syringe?"

"Oh, that's just a fancy word for the needle that you get a shot with."

Janice closed her eyes. "I know I said I wanted what would make Mom happy, but I don't think you should give her the medicine."

Her dad pulled his face away from hers. "No? Why not?"

Her eyes fluttered open. "Because it's never been tested. It could be dangerous. I read a story once about a boy who got shots that made him smart, the same shots a rat was getting. Everything was going fine until one day the rat died. That's when they knew the boy was gonna die too."

"Honey, that story was make-believe. This is real life."

Tears crawled slowly down Janice's cheeks. "Don't do it, Daddy. I don't want to lose Mom."

Her dad wiped her tears away with his thumb. "This is an adult decision, dear. I'm afraid it's up to your mother."

"You never listen to me when it's important," complained Janice.

"That's because the important decisions are not up to you; you're just a child. You'll understand when you get older."

Janice rolled over in her bed away from her father and faced the wall. "If something happens to her, I'll never forgive you."

He rose from the bed, turned out the light, and closed the door as he left.

***

The next day Dr. Cooper came home with a small box that contained a little bottle of serum and a needle to administer the experimental drug. His wife already had her sleeve rolled up when he walked in the door.

"Anxious to get started, I see," said Alan.

"I don't like needles so let's hurry and get this over with."

Alan poked the needle into the top of the serum and sucked some of it from the bottle with the syringe. Then he held the needle toward the ceiling and carefully pushed the plunger with his thumb to expel some of the mysterious liquid along with any air bubbles. A small stream of serum shot into the air until Alan was satisfied that all the air bubbles had been removed.

"Okay," said Alan, "here it goes."

Hilda turned her head away and closed her eyes. "Is it going to HURT?"

The last word of her question came out forcefully as the needle pierced her skin at that exact moment. She took a deep breath.

"All done," said Alan. He checked his watch and noted the time. "Six thirty, exactly."

"Hey, it's not like I'm one of your subjects," said Hilda.

"Actually, honey, you are ... secretly. This is all for science so we have to keep a close observation." He handed her a small red book and a pen. "Anytime you notice anything unusual, you need to write it down in this journal and also the time. Even if you don't, it's good to write in it every few hours or so, just to say how you're feeling."

Later that evening, Hilda wrote her first entry:

Dear journal, (Day 1, 9:53 p.m.)

It's been a little over three hours now, and I feel fine so far. I don't notice anything unusual at all. I can't wait to see what's going to happen. I wonder what kind of abilities I'm going to get. Alan only briefly mentioned that the rats in the lab were able to crawl through mazes without ever getting to a dead end, and some of them almost seemed to be able to float in the air. It would be so amazing if I could fly.

The next day while Janice was at school and Alan was at work, Hilda wrote again in her journal.

Dear Journal, (Day 2, 1:30 p.m.)

When is this dumb experiment going to take effect? I feel stupid running through the house and jumping, thinking I might be able to fly.

Later that evening, she wrote again.

Dear Journal, (Day 2, 8:45 p.m.)

I can feel them staring at me. Who? My family, of course. What kind of question was that? I feel like a giant rat. I see Alan staring at me and then writing in his own journal. I wonder what he's writing. Probably his Nobel Prize acceptance speech.

The next day:

Dear Journal, (Day 3, 11:30 a.m.)

Everyone is gone. Looks like another day of watching television. I don't feel weak, but I'm not going to get dressed today. I just don't feel like it. I'm just going to walk around in my bathrobe all day, if I decide to walk around at all.

Later that evening:

Dear Journal, (Day 3, 8:45 p.m.)

I think the family ate without me. I wasn't hungry anyway. My head has been hurting off and on most of the day. I wonder if I should tell Alan about it. It's probably nothing.

The next day Janice came home from school. The door to her house had been left open. She poked her head inside. "Mom, I'm home."

When she walked farther into the house, her jaw dropped. The kitchen cabinets were all opened, and there were torn boxes of food strewn all over the table and floor. It looked as if a bear had ransacked the place.

"Mom," she called, not too loud this time in case someone else was in the house instead like an intruder. She crept toward her mother's bedroom, almost afraid of what she might find. Pushing the door open with one finger, slowly the bed came into her view. She noticed her mom's legs on the bed first. They were halfway covered with her bathrobe. Finally, the door opened completely, and she could see her mom resting peacefully on the bed, lying flat on her back. Chocolate syrup was smeared on her face, and some food crumbs were sticking to it. Next to her was the red journal with the pen lodged inside.

Janice tiptoed into the room and carefully picked up the journal. She searched for the last entry. It read:

Dear Journal (Day 4, I think, sometime in the morning)

These headaches are making it harder and harder for me to think. I am hungry. I know that much. I feel like I'm losing my identity. I realize now I should have been happy just being Alan's wife or Janice's mom. Who am I now? What am I now? Ahhhh! The pain! It's too much! Can't take it anymore...............

Janice swallowed and put the book back down on the bed. It made a slight noise, enough to wake her mom. Hilda's eyes popped open, and her head jerked toward her daughter.

Janice reared back and shrieked.

Her mom's eyes contained a red zigzag pattern that made her look like a zombie or something.

"Mom, you're scaring me," cried Janice.

Her mom grabbed the journal and leaped from the bed. She shoved Janice aside and darted to the kitchen.

Janice stood there in shock, not knowing what to do. She could hear pots and pans clanging on the floor and cans of food being thrown against the wall. Cabinets were flinging open and shut. Slowly, Janice slid against the wall until she was sitting on the floor with her face in her hands while she wept. She cried for about three minutes straight until she noticed something peculiar. The house had grown quiet.

She rose from the carpet and peeked down the hall toward the kitchen. Was her mom still there? Cautiously, she walked down the hallway until she could see inside the kitchen. It was even messier than it was before. Now it looked like a couple of bears had gotten into a fight in there and the winner got to sift through the cabinets.

"Mother!" yelled Janice. "Where are you?"

The front door was still open, and Janice could hear car horns honking from outdoors. She dashed outside and looked far down the road from where the sounds were coming from. She recognized her mom in her bathrobe running across a busy intersection.

"Mom! Where are you going? Come back!"

And that was the last Janice saw of her mother.

Chapter 32

Janice, Bridgette, and her mom barged into Bridgette's house and locked the door behind them. The football game had just finished, and Mr. Swanson was pouring a cup of coffee.

"Why do you guys look like you're hiding from someone?" asked Mr. Swanson.

"It's my dad," replied Janice.

"Your dad?"

"Yeah, he thinks I'm going to turn into a Berserker."

"A what?"

"I'll explain it to you later, dear," said his wife.

"Look," said Bridgette. She was pointing at the television. A newswoman was reporting with a microphone in her hands.

"They're all over the city. We're calling them barrel towns. Several homeless people, mostly children, are gathering around metal barrels that have been set ablaze. Typically, there are 15 to 20 homeless gathered per barrel in alleys throughout our city, some upper class and some lower class neighborhoods. When we try to get an interview, they run from us. Only within the past few months have their numbers been increasing. Where are they coming from? We don't know. If you have any information, please call the number at the bottom of the screen."

"And to think, my dad is responsible for that," said Janice.

"There must be other classes," concluded Bridgette.

"What?" asked her father.

"There's too many of them to just be coming from our class, even if you add Wanda's class," added Bridgette.

"Which means they've been doing this for a while," said Janice.

"Or there are other experimental classes besides ours," said Bridgette.

***

The next day at school in room 333 George and Bridgette sat nervously after the bell rang. Knowing how Ms. Leadbetter felt about being late to class had them feeling uneasy since their teacher had not yet arrived.

Suddenly the door opened abruptly, and they jumped in their seats. Ms. Leadbetter, dressed in a navy blue business suit, barged through the door like she was on a mission. Quickly she turned toward her two students who were sitting together in the back row. "Good news! Your friend, Janice, was able to move her pencil today. She'll be joining us tomorrow. I told Tom and Cassandra if they can't move their pencils by tomorrow not to bother coming back at all.

"Now, let's get to a more pressing issue." Ms. Leadbetter glared at Bridgette. "Did you two really think you had me fooled? I've known what you've been up to for quite some time now."

"Exactly what is it that you think we've been up to?" asked Bridgette innocently.

"Don't be coy with me," warned Ms. Leadbetter while pointing at Bridgette. "The question you should be asking is What do I do with you now, now that you know that I know what you're up to?"

Ms. Leadbetter looked at the door that led to the hallway. "Nurse Meyers!"

The nurse, dressed in her white uniform, opened the door with a syringe in her hand. Carefully, she held it upright while she walked into the room toward Ms. Leadbetter.

Officer Halfpenny stepped into the room and blocked the door. He looked at Bridgette and George and pointed at them. While shaking his finger, he said, "I knowed that I would see you two again. I just knowed it."

"Ahhh, Nurse Meyers," began Ms. Leadbetter, "thank you for coming. I see you have our little surprise with you."

George started shaking in his seat. He glanced at Bridgette who slowly shook her head at him.

Ms. Leadbetter grinned at George. "George!"

The mere mention of his name from Ms. Leadbetter's shrill voice caused him to jump in his seat.

She continued. "I'm going to give you the option. Shall I inject this into you, or should I inject it into your friend?"

Nurse Meyers walked between the two students and waited for directions.

George gazed over at Bridgette. *What should I do?* he thought to Bridgette.

Bridgette didn't do or say anything.

"Wh what's in it?" asked George.

"Curious little thing," aren't you," snapped Ms. Leadbetter. "I suppose this means you choose yourself so you can find out what it is."

Bravely, George replied, "Yes, give it to me. That is what I desire."

"Desire?" Ms. Leadbetter laughed. "If you knew what was in it, you wouldn't *desire* it at all. Last chance. Are you sure you want us to give it to you and not your do-gooder friend?"

George looked at Bridgette fearfully. *Should I choose you?*

Bridgette bravely nodded and accepted her fate.

"Okay, give it to her!" screamed George. "I'm sorry, Bridgette! I'm sorry!" He blubbered like a baby.

"Too bad!" she yelled. "Did you actually think I was going to let you choose? How naïve of you." She chuckled a few times then gave Nurse Meyers the go-ahead nod.

Nurse Meyers stepped up and rolled up George's sleeve.

"Wait," said Bridgette.

Nurse Meyers stopped, and Ms. Leadbetter turned her head.

"You can't do this. It's not right."

All of a sudden she started to receive a vision. She couldn't quite make it out yet, but now was definitely not the time to zone out. Shapes started to take form. It was the weirdest thing she had ever experienced. It was like a movie playing in her head. One eye was viewing the movie while the other eye was watching what was going on in front of her. When she felt that she got the gist of the vision, she desperately shook her head and fought to stay in the moment.

Ms. Leadbetter nodded to Nurse Meyers. "Continue please."

The loyal nurse grabbed George's arm and pinched the skin where she was going to insert the needle.

Bridgette shook her head trying stubbornly to keep her futuristic vision at bay. She stared at the syringe intensely, and the vision disappeared.

Nurse Meyers' shot-giving hand began to tremble. Before she could stab the needle into George's arm, her arm involuntarily pivoted toward Ms. Leadbetter. She lunged out at Ms. Leadbetter, but the clever principal backed up in plenty of time to avoid the dissention.

"Ms. Leadbetter," gasped Nurse Meyers, "I ... I don't know what's going on. I was trying to give the shot to the boy."

"Don't worry, Nurse Meyers. We know exactly what's going on. Don't we, Bridgette?"

Bridgette stood from her chair. "If you think we're going to just sit here and let you poison us, then you're sadly mistaken!"

Ms. Leadbetter pulled some forms from behind the podium and waved them at Bridgette. "We have permission to *poison* you, sweety."

Bridgette concentrated on the signed documents, and they instantly ripped in half without Ms. Leadbetter's hands even moving.

"That's impressive, Bridgette, but we have other copies, and even if we didn't, there's no turning back now."

"Come on, George," commanded Bridgette, "we're leaving."

George stood, and together he and Bridgette walked toward the door where Officer Halfpenny was waiting with his arms folded.

"Goin somewheres?" said Officer Halfpenny smugly.

Bridgette made a sweeping motion with her hand, and the security guard stumbled to his left away from the door.

"What the heck!" he hollered. He reached for his taser.

Bridgette was one step ahead of him. She waved her arm again, and the gun lifted out of its holster and flew against the wall across the room.

Ms. Leadbetter slapped her hands together excitedly and placed them against her bottom lip. "I knew it. She's been holding back."

Once Bridgette and George left the room, Officer Halfpenny said, "I'll go fetch 'em."

"No," demanded Ms. Leadbetter, "I got what I wanted for today."

"But they fixin to excape."

Ms. Leadbetter glared at him. "We don't pay you to question my authority. Now go back to whatever it is that you do here."

"Yes, ma'am."

Ms. Leadbetter tapped her fingers against her chin, deep in thought.

Chapter 33

Ms. Leadbetter walked into her office and sat down with a cup of coffee. Her peaceful moment was shattered by a buzzing noise.

"Yes, Sheila, what is it?"

"Sorry to bother you, Jane, but a Mrs. Olson is here to see you."

"Send her in," groaned Ms. Leadbetter.

The door opened, and Mrs. Olson stepped into the room. She was dressed in purple pants with a matching blouse. Her dark hair was pinned up, stacked like a wedding cake.

"Have a seat Mrs. Olson," said Ms. Leadbetter.

"Oh, please, call me Judy."

Ms. Leadbetter forced a smile.

"I'll get right to the point. As you know, working at the orphanage for all these years has given me a fondness for my job. Conducting risky *illegal* things could jeopardize my career, not to mention my freedom-"

"I thought you said you'd get right to the point," interrupted Ms. Leadbetter. "Never mind, I know why you're here. I'm not giving you more than the agreed upon rate for each snot-nosed kid you bring me, and don't try to threaten me with going to the authorities as we both know you wouldn't do that. We're both guilty of doing illegal activities with these children. Now, where are the five *little darlings* that you have for me today?"

"They're with Officer Halfpenny in the security office as always," replied Judy.

Ms. Leadbetter handed an envelope full of cash. "Here you go, five hundred dollars per head. That's twenty-five hundred dollars."

Mrs. Olson took the money and asked, "What happens to these children?"

Ms. Leadbetter crinkled her eyebrows and said, "As a teacher and the principal at this school, I am the one who does all the questioning here. Let's just stick with our little arrangement and leave it at that, shall we?"

Mrs. Olson stood. "Very well, I'll see you in a couple of weeks with another group of kids."

Ms. Leadbetter gave a quick wave. "Bye now."

***

The cafeteria was its typical noisy self. The herd of students nibbled bits of food in between loud conversations.

Among the chaos was Wanda and her crew sitting at no particular table.

Bridgette, George, and Janice walked up to the table and sat down.

"How are you doing?" asked Bridgette to Wanda.

"Okay, I guess," she replied.

"No, what I mean is, how are you *feeling*?" asked Bridgette.

Not used to such caring questions, Wanda seemed a bit dazed but then answered, "I'm a bit worried, of course, but I'm also hopeful." She smiled.

Bridgette smiled too.

I wonder why she's not asking how I'm feeling, thought Cathy.

Bridgette looked at Cathy. "Sorry, Cathy, I care about you too; it's just that, well, you know, Wanda's sister and all."

Cathy looked confused. "Wanda's sister?"

Wanda glanced at Bridgette and shook her head. *Please don't tell her.*

"Oh, nothing important," replied Bridgette. "What we need to talk about though is Ms. Leadbetter."

Wanda and her girls leaned forward.

Bridgette continued. "She knows now about my abilities."

"All of them?" asked Janice.

"Well, I'm not sure how much she knows. She just saw me use them to leave her class today, and I was much more forceful

168

than she had been led to believe. She knows I've been holding back."

"So now what?" asked Wanda.

"Things are happening quickly," said Bridgette. "We're about to have an all-out war here at the school."

"I think you're exaggerating, Bridgette," said Wanda.

Bridgette shook her head. "No, it's us against them."

"How do you know?" asked Wanda.

"I've seen it."

"Huh?" Wanda looked confused.

Bridgette leaned in toward the table. "Sometimes I get glimpses of the future."

Wanda's mouth dropped open.

Cathy said, "That's impossible. Nobody can do that."

Maria chimed in as well. "There's no class for that here. How do you know it's the future you're seeing?"

"Each time I've had a vision, up to about a day later, it starts to come true, but it can be altered if we try to change it."

Wanda shook her head. "Dang, is there anything you can't do?"

"You believe her?" asked Maria in disbelief.

"You've seen what she can do," responded Wanda. "She also has *our* power as well."

"Imagine all this power in the hands of Ms. Leadbetter," said George. "We have to protect Bridgette from her."

"I think Bridgette can protect herself," replied Wanda.

"Thanks for your confidence in me," said Bridgette, "but I'm afraid I may be overmatched here, especially if my vision comes true. If only Ms. Leadbetter didn't know about my powers."

"What if she wasn't sure?" asked Wanda.

"What do you mean?" replied Bridgette.

"Do you mean.....?" started Maria.

And then Maria, Cathy, and Wanda all simultaneously said, "The recurring nightmare."

"The what?" asked Bridgette.

"Recurring means it happens over and over again," said George.

Janice slapped him in the head. "We know that, genius."

George slid had hand over his head like he was smoothing down his hair.

"I guess I meant 'how does it work?'" said Bridgette. "Sorry, George." She glanced at Janice pleadingly.

"Well," began Wanda, "it will take a lot of practice to pull this off, but the way it works is that we keep giving Ms. Leadbetter the same dream over and over again about her watching you use your powers the same way you used them today. By the time she wakes up, she will have had the same dream at least 50 times. Then she won't be able to tell if what she saw you do today really happened or if it was all part of her dream."

"That's brilliant," said Bridgette, "and deceptive."

"Funny you should say that," replied Wanda. "This is just the beginning of the deception. You and George will need to continue deceiving her at school when you act like today never happened."

Bridgette and Wanda both looked at George as if he might be the weakest link.

"What?" said George defensively. "We don't just have to act the part; we have to think it as well. Remember, she can read our minds."

Bridgette looked concerned. "Are you saying you won't be able to do it, Whiz?"

Hearing the word, Whiz, made him get the tingles. He smiled and said, "I didn't say that. I just think we need to make a plan that will help us not think about the deception."

"Music!" hollered Cathy.

They all turned her way and waited for the explanation.

"Put an earbud in one ear with music playing. While you're listening to the music, you can sing the song in your head while listening to what's going on in the classroom at the same time."

"That idea is music to my ears," beamed Bridgette.

"Corny," said Janice with a high pitched tone. Then she corrected herself. "Not your idea, Cathy. I was talking about Bridgette's little "music-to-my-ears" comment."

They all laughed.

"Corny, yes," said Bridgette, "but sincere. Good idea, Cathy. We really need this to work so we can buy some more time to train."

"I know," said George. "I can almost lift my bed now just by concentrating for a few seconds."

Janice lightly punched George's shoulder. "Now if you could just learn to breathe while doing it, you might stop passing out half the time."

"Okay, will you guys be able to meet at my place later tonight?" asked Bridgette.

"Hey," responded Wanda, "like you said, it's an all-out war, us against them."

***

That evening they rehearsed the Leadbetter scene over and over until they didn't even have to think about their lines. Maria and Cathy played the parts of Nurse Meyers and Ms. Leadbetter.

It was past midnight by the time they were all satisfied. That's when Wanda went to work. Once everyone was asleep, she pulled them all into the same dream, Ms. Leadbetter's nightmare, where they acted out their roles again and again. Because it was Wanda's created dream, she had to stay out of sight as she was not a character in the original event. She waited in the hallway until George and Bridgette would come barging out. Then she would rewind the dream and start it up again, making sure Ms. Leadbetter was exposed to the same recurring dream all night long.

Chapter 34

Bridgette, George, and Janice waited patiently in room 333 the following morning. They were to think only curious thoughts about what their training would be like today. They couldn't think about the confrontation George and Bridgette had with Ms. Leadbetter the day before, or they would ruin the entire night's worth of recurring nightmare trickery. When in doubt, sing the words to the song playing in one of their ears, thanks to Cathy's idea.

Ten minutes after the bell, they heard the eerie footsteps of Ms. Leadbetter clomping toward them on the hard polished floor, a bit faster than usual.

Moments later they stopped outside the door.

George could feel himself holding his breath while still keeping curious thoughts about what training he would get today.

The doorknob slowly turned, and the door flew open.

Ms. Leadbetter, dressed in a black business suit, with her black briefcase in her hand, glared at them and shouted, "What are you three doing in here?"

Bridgette spoke for them. "You told us yesterday that we should start meeting you here from now on. We thought we were supposed to come in and wait … like in the other class."

Ms. Leadbetter turned her head slightly and stared at her from the corners of her eyes as if she were thinking back in time, trying to remember her own words. She lowered her voice and said suspiciously, "And what were the words I used?"

"Gosh, I don't remember them exactly, but it was something like to start meeting in room 333 from now on to continue our training." She glanced at George. "Right, George?"

George nodded while thinking in his mind, *I hope I learn a lot today.*

Ms. Leadbetter shook her head and said, "You'll have to forgive me; I didn't get a lot of sleep last night." She looked at

Janice. "I see you made it to the right room, Janice. I'll bet your father is very proud of you."

"He is," replied Janice. "Does he work near here? I mean, do you see much of him?"

"Ah ah ah," warned Ms. Leadbetter. "Remember who asks the questions around here."

"Yes, Ma'am," said Janice quickly.

Ms. Leadbetter cleared her throat. "I haven't seen your father in weeks, to tell you the truth. He works in the lab. *You* know that. That's an entirely different building across the parking lot.

"Speaking of across the parking lot, we have a special field trip today."

"A field trip?" asked Bridgette.

"Now Bridgette," began Ms. Leadbetter, "That almost sounded like a question, but I'll let it pass as merely something a parrot might do."

Bridgette smiled nervously. She couldn't think about whether Ms. Leadbetter was up to something or not, none of them could. It might give away the whole cover up they worked so hard for. She hummed a few of the words of the song playing in her ear.

Ms. Leadbetter placed her briefcase on a desk and opened it. After shuffling through some papers, she said, "Oh, dear, I left your parents' signed field trip permission slips in my office. Wait right here. I'll be back in a jiffy. I know George would like to see his before we leave." She gave George a huge wicked grin, opened the door, and walked out into the long corridor sounding like a horse clomping its shoes in a parade.

Bridgette tried to read Ms. Leadbetter's mind while she walked away.

Something's not right, thought Ms. Leadbetter. *Those kids just might be up to something. I can't take any chances. I'm going to have to..............*

And that was all Bridgette could get before Ms. Leadbetter was too far away to mind-read.

George's nervous smile disappeared when the door closed behind their teacher. He leaned toward the girls. "Field trip?" he whispered. "Is she telling the truth?"

Bridgette scanned the room. "It could have something to do with our training," she suggested. "This room doesn't look much different than our Mind over Matter classroom so I'm not sure why we would even meet here."

When she figured Ms. Leadbetter was far enough away that their minds couldn't be read, Bridgette whispered, "I think she's on to us. I could hear her thoughts, and they're not good. She was thinking about not taking any chances with us and that she was going to have to do something, but I couldn't tell what it was, but it doesn't sound good."

George pulled the phone from his pocket. "That's it, I'm calling my mom to ask about this so called field trip." He pressed some numbers and held the phone up to his ear. After a few seconds, he said, "Dang! No Answer." So he texted his mother a quick message: DO YOU KNOW ABOUT MS. LEADBETTER TAKING US ON A FIELD TRIP TODAY?

"What should we do?" asked Janice.

"Maybe we should just go home," suggested George.

"No," commanded Bridgette, "we need to stick together. We can't separate. We're stronger when we're together."

"But we could be walking into a trap," said George.

"Trust me," said Bridgette. "If we separate, she'll try to pick us apart one-by-one. Remember, George. Courage. Let's walk like lions. She's unsure right now, so I don't think she's going to do anything outrageous. Besides she needs us, or we wouldn't be here getting abilities for free."

"But what does she need us for?" asked Janice.

"That's the million dollar question," replied George.

Suddenly, the echo of Ms. Leadbetter's footsteps clip-clopping down the hall came to within hearing distance.

"She's coming," whispered Bridgette. "Remember, listen to your music and sing along if you have to. Don't give us away, and just follow my lead."

Ms. Leadbetter opened the door and said, "Okay, let's go. We'll just walk across the parking lot. No need to take a school van." She held up a permission slip and showed it to George. "Would you like to see your parents' permission slip, or shall I hold onto it?"

George smiled nervously and shook his head while trying to concentrate on the words to the song he was listening to.

They walked across the parking lot past a section of parked cars and entered an adjacent building to their school.

Ms. Leadbetter held out one hand like a model might do when showing some merchandise for sale. "This is Dr. Alan Cooper's laboratory. Janice, you may know him as *Dad*."

Startled by the unscheduled visit, Dr. Cooper stood from his desk chair and said, "What a surprise! You've brought my daughter and some of her friends to visit." He glanced at Ms. Leadbetter, and she and Bridgette both read his mind.

Why have you brought them here. I don't want my daughter to find out.

"I thought you all might like to see what Dr. Cooper is working on," said Ms. Leadbetter.

Are you crazy? thought Dr. Cooper. *Get them out of here.*

"Let's show them the rats," suggested Ms. Leadbetter. "This way, students, right through this door."

Janice looked at her father and glared. "Look, Dad, I'm still a person," spat Janice sarcastically. She turned away and followed the group into the warehouse. He followed close behind.

The warehouse was huge. Hundreds of feet stretched out in front of them full of tables and cages.

"Uh, how would you guys like to feed some rats?" asked Dr. Cooper.

"Cool," responded George.

Janice and Bridgette didn't say anything. They just kept walking, following Ms. Leadbetter who was walking toward a bunch of tables with metal rat cages on top of them.

Mr. Cooper dug in the little refrigerator under one of the tables and pulled up a small chunk of cheese. He opened up the glass cage that contained a maze and a rat. On the end where the maze ended he placed the cheese. "Watch."

The rat lifted its nose and sniffed the air. It knew there was cheese nearby. Instead of trying to solve the maze to reach its prize, it floated upward toward the ceiling of its cage and then swam through the air toward the cheese. When it reached its reward, it descended and grabbed the cheese between its paws and started nibbling on it.

"This is where it all started," said Dr. Cooper.

Not quite, thought Ms. Leadbetter, and Bridgette heard her thoughts.

Not quite? thought Bridgette. *What does that mean?*

Bridgette didn't realize what she was thinking until Ms. Leadbetter turned and stared at her with wide eyes.

Oh, great, thought Bridgette, *now you know.*

Of course, I know thought Ms. Leadbetter. *Who do you think created the recurring nightmare to cause uncertainty? It was a valiant attempt, but you can't trick someone with their own deception.*

So why are we here? asked Bridgette.

Finally, George caught on to what was going on. He looked at Ms. Leadbetter and then at Bridgette. "Do you guys want to let us in on the conversation?"

"Sure," replied Bridgette. "She knows."

"She knows what?" asked George.

"She knows I can read her mind. She knows about my powers."

"All of them?" asked George.

"She knows her nightmare the other night was used to try to cover up the powers she saw me use," said Bridgette.

"Which reminds me," said Ms. Leadbetter. "Did you do that on your own, or did you have help from one of Mr. Pleasant's students? After all, that's one of their specialties."

"Don't tell her anything, Bridgette," blurted Janice.

Ms. Leadbetter looked back at Dr. Cooper. "You need to control your daughter."

Dr. Cooper was speechless. His face was full of worry.

Bridgette looked at him and tried to read his mind.

"Well," began Ms. Leadbetter, "I think I have no choice but to give up our secret. I know you don't trust me, so what if I show you what we're hiding behind that door over there?" She pointed across the room at a single red door on the far side of the wall.

"It's a trap," said George.

Bridgette shook her head. "No, I don't think it is."

"How do you know?" asked Janice.

She turned toward Dr. Cooper. "Ask *him* how I know."

Dr. Cooper directed his eyes at Ms. Leadbetter. "You can't take them back there. No one can know. It could jeopardize all my work as a scientist."

"Sorry, Al, but we need them to trust us. They are vital to our work."

Ms. Leadbetter started marching toward the red door.

Dr. Cooper held out his hands. "Please, I beg of you. If not for my work, then do this to spare my daughter."

Ms. Leadbetter scoffed at the remark. "Ha, your daughter is stronger than you think. She can take it. In fact, she'll probably thank me for it."

Dr. Cooper ran in front of Ms. Leadbetter to stop her from reaching the door.

Ms. Leadbetter smiled and slowly lifted one arm in the air.

Dr. Cooper's body lifted off the ground and rose toward the ceiling, his legs kicking frantically. "Let me down!"

Bridgette felt sorry for him. She locked her eyes on him and lowered her head toward the ground. Immediately, he began descending.

Ms. Leadbetter looked at Bridgette and gave a wicked smile as if she liked what she saw.

By the time Dr. Cooper reached the floor, Ms. Leadbetter had grabbed a hold of the doorknob to the red door.

Bridgette could only think that the color red meant stop or danger.

Chapter 35

"Right this way," said Ms. Leadbetter. She turned the doorknob and leaned into the heavy red door. They all walked through the doorway.

On the other side of the door was a small hallway sandwiched between two walls where an elevator stood waiting patiently.

Ms. Leadbetter swaggered up to the elevator and pushed the button shaped like an arrow pointing downward. It lit up after she pressed it, and the elevator doors opened followed by the dinging of a bell.

"Everybody in," ordered Ms. Leadbetter."Time to check out the basement where the *bigger* lab rats live." She put extra emphasis on the word "bigger" as if it were meaningful for some reason.

"Ms. Leadbetter, please," pleaded Dr. Cooper. "It's not too late to stop this."

"Give me a break!" screeched Ms. Leadbetter. "Have you seen your child lately? Not exactly a "pleased-to-meet-you" kind of girl. If anything, this will most likely help her."

They all followed Ms. Leadbetter into the elevator. She pressed the "B" for basement with one of her long freshly painted fingernails. The doors carefully closed. They could hear a slight humming noise while the elevator descended slowly. They jerked to a halt, and the doors opened once again.

Ms. Leadbetter stepped out first. "Right this way ladies and gentlemen."

She led them around a corner to a room about the size of a 40 by 40 foot box. In the center sat a 10 by 10 by 10 foot transparent cube. A bed was positioned in the corner, but it was empty. Beside the bed, cuddled into a ball on the floor, a woman lay sleeping. On the other side of the cube stood a lone toilet.

"Who's that woman?" asked George.

They couldn't see her face because her head was down and huddled into her chest.

"Okay, they've seen her," said Dr. Cooper. "Let's get out of here."

"Feed her!" demanded Ms. Leadbetter.

Dr. Cooper thought in his mind, *You stupid little...-*

"Really, Dr. Cooper," interrupted Ms. Leadbetter. "I thought childish thoughts like those were beneath you."

Dr. Cooper sighed and said, "What should I feed her?"

"I don't know. Get her a breakfast food."

Dr. Cooper walked over to a cabinet, opened it, and pulled out a packaged pastry. He unwrapped it and placed it on a small plate. He transferred it into a small microwave that was on the counter.

"Is that really necessary?" asked Ms. Leadbetter, running out of patience.

"She likes her pastries warmed up," he replied.

"Really?" said Ms. Leadbetter. "And did she tell you this?"

Dr. Cooper removed the plated pastry from the microwave and walked over to the transparent door to the cube. There was a large gap between the bottom of the door and the floor. He placed the plate on the floor and slid it into the room with the woman.

"Watch this," said Ms. Leadbetter. "We don't even have to wake her."

The woman began to stir. Her messy long strands of hair were covering her face, but she lifted her nose in the air to get a whiff of the warm pastry. Instinctively, she rolled to her hands and knees and began crawling toward the smell. When she reached the pastry, she hungrily snatched it up in her hands and started stuffing it in her mouth, along with her locks of hair. While chewing, she grabbed a handful of hair from her mouth and then moved it to the side of her head. That's when she noticed she was being watched. She lifted her head to expose her bloodshot eyes with little red veins zigzagging through them.

Janice's mouth gaped open. "Mom!"

179

Dr. Cooper winced as if he were hoping she wouldn't figure it out.

Janice looked over at her dad.

"I can explain, honey," said Dr. Cooper.

Janice folded her arms and glared.

Ms. Leadbetter grinned and stood in silence as she watched the father-daughter confrontation commence.

"I'm waiting," said Janice angrily.

"What did you expect me to do?" asked Dr. Cooper rhetorically. "Bring her home so she could run away again? This is the best place for her where I can keep an eye on her.....keep her safe from the world.....and herself."

"You have her caged like an animal," said Janice with a disgusted tone.

"Well, honey, she's acting like an animal. Would you like to live in a house with a wild bear running loose in it? This is the perfect place for her because I can keep her safe while I continue working on an antidote to reverse the effects of the drug."

"The drug that *you* gave her," spat Janice.

"Honey, you know I tried to tell her no," pleaded her father.

"Yeah, I could tell you were all bent out of shape, especially when you handed her that journal with a smile. You were glad to begin experimenting on her."

"I hate to interrupt this family matter," said Ms. Leadbetter, "but I think we've seen enough." She turned toward Bridgette. "Now you know what we're trying to do. We're working on an antidote to cure this horrible side effect for our duds."

"Duds?" said Bridgette. "These people have names. You treat them like they're disposable or something. You could at least call them *failed experiments*. But no, you wouldn't call them that because that would make it look like *you* failed them instead of them being the ones that failed."

Ms. Leadbetter's eyebrows cringed. "Throwing blame around like that does not change the facts. We are trying to cure these people."

"This doesn't answer the big question though," said Bridgette. "Why are you doing these experiments in the first place?"

Ms. Leadbetter held up her finger. "Ah, ah, ah, Bridgette, remember who asks the questions around here."

"How convenient," said Bridgette. "You always spit that phrase at us when you don't want to tell us something."

"Did you think I brought you on this field trip today to tell you everything?" asked Ms. Leadbetter. "When you are the principal of your own school, then you too can be privy to all the information. Information is power, and I *have* all the power. Why would I share it with you?"

Bridgette took two steps backward. "You did share it with me, remember?" She raised her hands in the air, and Ms. Leadbetter began floating upward.

Bridgette turned toward George and Janice. "Run to the elevator. We're getting out of here."

The two of them bolted back the way they came.

Ms. Leadbetter laughed while being suspended in air. "Bridgette, darling, you are no match for me." She held her arms out by her sides and concentrated. Slowly, she descended toward to the floor. She hit the ground chasing after them.

"Oh yeah?" replied Bridgette. She concentrated on Dr. Cooper and forced him to stagger in Ms. Leadbetter's path. They collided, and both stumbled to the floor.

Bridgette turned and sprinted toward the elevator and her friends. George was holding the door open with one hand grasped onto the side.

Once Bridgette was safely inside, George released the door, and it began stubbornly closing slow and deliberate-like. They could all see Ms. Leadbetter stand in a hurry while the doctor stayed on the floor. Ms. Leadbetter's eyes had an evil glow to them while she raced toward the fugitives.

As if the door could hear him, George shouted, "Hurry up, you stupid door!" He pressed both hands on the metal door, one on either side, and tried to squeeze them together. It was no use; the doors were going to close when they wanted to.

Ms. Leadbetter was halfway there, not fast enough to reach them in time, but close enough to use her power. She raised both hands and made a motion like she was opening invisible elevator doors. The doors suddenly slowed down and stopped closing.

George continued trying to squeeze the doors shut. A bead of sweat rolled off his forehead. "Bridgette," he grunted, "the doors are starting to open!"

Bridgette held her arms outward and then focused on bringing her hands together. The doors followed her movement and slowly started shutting. Almost like there was an invisible force between her hands, Bridgette struggled to make her hands touch. Her body trembled. She stretched her fingers toward each other, only inches away from touching, just the like door, only inches away from closing.

"I got this," said George. While staring at Ms. Leadbetter, he tried to make her legs trip over each other. He was unsuccessful, but he managed to make her catch herself from falling and lose focus for just a second, enough to loosen her hold on the door so that it could close all the way.

Bridgette's fingers touched, and she blew out a sigh of relief. "That was close."

George noticed first. "Hey, we're not moving!" He glanced up at the two buttons on the wall. The "B" and the "1" were both darkened. "Press the "1!" Press the "1!"

Janice lunged at the button like she was playing a game of Family Feud or something. The "1" lit up, and the elevator started its slow ascent back to the first floor.

They all leaned against the back wall to catch their breath.

"Come on! Come on!" urged George, trying to speed up the elevator's sluggish movement.

After what seemed to be minutes but was only mere seconds, the elevator stopped.

They waited for the doors to open, but they wouldn't. The elevator began to shake.

"Now what?" said Janice.

The light on the "1" was still lit, but suddenly, the elevator started shuttering

"Uh," uttered George, "I think she's pulling us down."

"Is she that strong?" asked Janice.

"I guess we don't really know *how* strong she is," said Bridgette.

George turned to Bridgette. "What do we do now?"

Bridgette clapped her hands together and stared at the door. While slowly pulling her palms apart, the doors simultaneously began to spread. They could see that the first floor and the elevator floor were not even. The elevator floor was dropping in a herky-jerky motion.

Without being told, George said, "It's now or never." He jumped upward an extra foot so that he could land flatly on the first floor. Janice followed. By the time Bridgette was able to leap, the elevator had fallen another foot. Janice and George motioned with their hands for Bridgette to leap, and she did. Her friends grabbed each of her arms to catch her and make sure she cleared the jump.

"Let's get out of here," said Bridgette. They darted out the red door, across the laboratory, and out of the building.

The elevator doors opened up again on the basement level. Ms. Leadbetter was standing there, waiting to have a battle of the minds with Bridgette. When she saw that the elevator was empty, she gave a big sigh of disappointment.

Dr. Cooper walked up to her and asked, "Did they get away?"

Ms. Leadbetter grinned. "For the moment."

Good, thought Dr. Cooper.

"Don't think that I didn't hear that."

"I'm just worried about my daughter," said Alan.

"She is the least of my concerns and should be of yours as well. If I were you, I'd be more worried about getting your wife back."

Chapter 36

Bridgette pulled out her phone while she, George, and Janice jogged toward home. She pushed a few buttons and waited. "Mom, where are you?"

Pause.

"Great! We're on our way home. Please come and get us as fast as you can. It's me, Janice, and George. We'll be heading your way on your side of the street. It's an emergency."

Pause.

"I can't explain right now. Are you in the car yet? Hurry, please."

After about five minutes of running and looking over their shoulders, the three students were picked up by Bridgette's mother.

Bridgette explained what had happened.

"We're calling the police," replied Mrs. Swanson.

"They're not going to believe your story," cried Bridgette.

"*I* wouldn't believe it," agreed George.

"We have to try," said Janice. "I don't really care much for the police, but we need some people on our side."

"You're right," agreed Bridgette. "Guys, I have the perfect plan. Ole Leadbottom's going down tonight."

Bridgette explained her elaborate scheme to everyone in the car. When she was done, her mom said, "It sounds so dangerous."

"Mom, the police will be there, right? After all, that's your job."

Mrs. Swanson gripped the steering wheel tightly and nodded.

Bridgette turned to Janice. "A lot hinges on you though, Janice. Will you do it?"

"You got us this far, Bridge," replied Janice. "George and I are not about to back down now."

George gulped. "Hey, speak for yourself."

I can't do this. It's too dangerous, he thought.

Bridgette had read George's mind.

"George, you don't have to do this," said Bridgette.

"Are you kidding?" said Janice. "George has more guts than all of us. I've been saying that all along. Walk like lions, right George?"

George nodded. "Wouldn't miss it for the world."

Was that brave……or stupid? thought George.

"Glad you still got your guts, Whiz." Janice slugged him in the stomach affectionately.

Bridgette placed her hand on George's shoulder. "You just be careful around any tiny airplanes."

"What does that mean?" asked George.

"They're more dangerous than they look; that's all."

Mrs. Swanson pulled into Bridgette's driveway, and they all exited the vehicle.

"Okay," said Bridgette, "Janice, call your dad. Remember, tell him we want to meet him in the lab at midnight. Mom, call the police; George, stay here and practice your powers, and I'll call Wanda and then try to contact the Alpha later tonight in his dreams."

They stormed into the house, but it didn't stop Bridgette's dad from watching the ball game on TV.

The kids ran to Bridgette's bedroom to carry out their tasks.

"Everything okay, dear?" called out Mr. Swanson.

Mrs. Swanson pulled out her cell phone "It will be." She dialed 911. "Hello, I'd like to give an anonymous tip."

"Go ahead," said the voice on the other line.

"Something really bad is going to happen at the Las Vegas School of Excellence tonight at midnight."

"I'm patching you in to the Las Vegas precinct right now. Go ahead, Sergeant Davenport."

"Hello, this is Sergeant Davenport. Who am I speaking to?"

"I don't want to give my name, if that' okay," responded Mrs. Swanson. "I just wanted you to know that there is going to

185

be trouble at midnight tonight in the lab at the Las Vegas School of Excellence."

"And how do you know this, Miss?"

"I just know. Please have some officers present. They're going to need you."

"We'll take it into consideration, Miss…..uh, are you sure you don't want to give your name?"

"I'm sure."

"Okay, well then, thank you for the call."

The sergeant hung up his phone but then dialed a number right afterwards. "Officer Halfpenny, I just got an interesting phone call about your neck of the woods. Sounds like something's goin' down in the lab around midnight tonight."

Pause.

"Hey, no problem. Say hi to the Mrs…….Peace out."

***

At nine o'clock that evening Officer Halfpenny made a phone call. "Hey, Charlie, you ready to make some mo' easy money?"

Pause.

"Nah, ain't nothin' like that this time, although I do love watching them kids roll in the street. Nah, we just gonna do some reconnaissance at the lab about midnight. Might even get to test those new planes we was bein' trained on. You know they ten times stronger than our tasers, don't you? Illegal in the U.S."

Pause.

"Oh, she'll pay us plenty. She always tellin' me to mind my own bitness, but every time I get involved, my wallet git a little bit thicker."

Pause.

"Alright, meet me in the office 'bout five of…….. Peace."

Chapter 37

With George and Janice still hanging out in her room, Bridgette lay on her bed facing the ceiling. It was one hour before midnight and her last attempt to try and reach the Alpha in his dreams. She had already been unsuccessful twice that night because he wasn't asleep. She closed her eyes and focused on the Alpha.

When she opened her eyes again, she was in a dark alley, one she didn't recognize. She noticed the familiar fiery barrel blowing ashes and red burning embers up into the black sky. But where was the Alpha? This was unusual as she had always transported directly to the vicinity of her desired subject. She knew she had nothing to fear, though the place was rather eerie.

She didn't even know his name so she called out, "Uh….. Alpha?"

No response, at least not one she could hear or see.

Losing her patience because she was short on time, Bridgette cupped her hands around her mouth and shouted out a supersonic scream. "ALPHAAAA!!!!"

The sheer force of her breath caused the flames in the barrel to flicker wildly inside, almost putting out the fire completely.

Without warning, a pair of dirty hands emerged from the darkness like a sneaky shark attack. They grabbed ahold of Bridgette's neck from behind and started tightening, trying to cut off the circulation of blood to her head so she would pass out.

Startled at first, Bridgette gasped for air while trying to pry the thick arms loose from around her neck. Eventually, she regained her senses and realized that she couldn't be hurt in her own fabricated dream.

Bridgette said aloud, "I know that's you, Alpha. Let me know when you're done choking me so we can talk. I'm inside another one of your dreams. Well, actually, I pulled you into one of my dreams. You're asleep, but I need you to wake up. We need your help."

Prove it, thought the Alpha.

Bridgette, with the Alpha still attached to her neck, shuffled her feet toward the barrel of fire. Instead of burning him this time, she reached into the leaping flames and grabbed a long mop handle that was on fire from top to bottom. She held it in her hands, and nothing happened. It did not burn her one bit.

Seeing the Alpha was not too impressed, she lifted the mop handle high in the air and put one end in her mouth while shoving the flaming stick down her throat. She licked her fingers and said, "Mmm, tasty."

The Alpha tried to tighten his grip. *Saw that one before.*

"Are you kidding me?" cried Bridgette. She pulled the extinguished stick from her mouth, smoke pouring off of it. "Well, have you seen this one?" She straddled the stick like a horse and shouted, "Giddy up!" She and the Alpha, who was also sitting on the stick, flew upward into the sky. They circled the small barrel town and landed back near the barrel.

The Alpha released his choke hold on Bridgette and thought, *Thanks for not burning me this time.*

"Sure," said Bridgette. She got right to the point. "Remember how I said we might be able to help each other?"

The Alpha nodded.

"Well, tonight it's all going down. It's us against them, and we're going to win. The people responsible for turning you into what you are will be in the lab in less than an hour from now. Will you fight with us?"

Can they change me back?

"Well, I can't make any promises," admitted Bridgette, "but I'm hoping and praying that they can. I know they're working on a cure."

I'll do it.

"Great, it's at the lab next to the Las Vegas School of Excellence."

I know the place well.

"Be there at midnight.

"Wait....you're asleep. We need to wake you up so you can get there on time."

I'll do it this time. He reached inside the burning barrel until his arm caught on fire.

Seconds later, while lying in the dark next to a fiery barrel and other Berserkers, the Alpha's eyes shot open. With a look of determination, he stood and began an evenly paced trot toward the school......by himself.

Chapter 38

Bridgette woke from her dream weaving episode. "He's on his way," she declared.

George and Janice both looked relieved and gave each other a high five.

"That should do it then," said Janice. "Your mom warned the police, Wanda said she'd show, and the alpha will be there for backup."

"What about your dad?" asked Bridgette, still trying to wake completely from her nap.

"Yep, he acted like he was *really* concerned about me and said he'd be there *by himself.* Yeah, right. We all know he told Ms. Leadbottom."

"We're counting on it," said Bridgette.

"Remind me why we didn't ask him to tell Ms. Leadbetter to be there," said Janice.

"I got this, Bridge," responded George. "See, Janice, if we told him to tell Ms. Leadbetter to come, she'd know we would be expecting her to be there. By trying to tell him to meet us alone, Ms. Leadbetter will think that *we* think he'll be alone so that way she can get the drop on us. She thinks we won't suspect her hiding there to get us."

"After all," said Bridgette, "we're only kids. How could we be so clever?" She smiled and winked.

"What about our parents?" asked George. "Shouldn't we tell them?"

"My parents already know," replied Bridgette.

"And my dad already knows too, of course," responded Janice.

"And my mom's not going," said Bridgette. "She feels safer now that she's called the police and asked them to be there."

"I don't know," said George. "If my parents knew what was going on, I don't think they would let me go. They wouldn't even consider it."

"Which is why, Whiz," said Janice, "you shouldn't tell them. We need you there tonight and your powers."

"Yeah, but I didn't get a lot of time to practice. I'm no stronger than yesterday."

Janice placed her hand on his shoulder. "Don't worry; we have our secret weapon." She glanced at Bridgette. "Just knowing Bridgette will be there should give us all the courage of a lion."

Bridgette smiled, but it was a nervous grin. She hadn't told any of them about the helmet that was attached to her head in one of her previous visions. She just hoped that the knowledge of it was enough to prevent it from happening. She knew it would happen tonight though. The lab was the same place in her vision, and she had a strong feeling that the present was catching up fast with the future encounter.

"Okay," said Bridgette, "I think it's time to go."

George shook his head nervously. "I need insurance."

Janice and Bridgette both looked confused.

"Elaborate, please," said Bridgette.

"Well, just think about it," explained George. "We have access to a human time machine that can see into the future. I want to know that we all make it out of this okay."

"We can't pinpoint the time, George," said Bridgette. "It's a great idea, but we're running out of time too. We can't be late to our own ambush."

"Let's just try once," suggested Janice.

Bridgette checked the clock on the wall. It was 11:25. "One try," she agreed.

"Okay," said Janice. "Here's something that should make you mad enough to have a futuristic vision: You know my dad is going to double-cross us tonight by telling Ms. Leadbetter that we're coming. It's going to be all his fault."

Though it wasn't enough to cause a vision to occur, Bridgette had to make a quick decision. She was going to have to lie in order to save the night.

Bridgette stared at the wall as if she were in a trance.

George whispered to Janice, "It's working."

Two minutes later Bridgette blinked and relaxed. She smiled and said, "It's going to be okay."

George brightened up. "What did you see?"

Bridgette smiled as if she could still see the image in her mind. "Well, the three of us were leaving the store with ice cream cones in our hands. It was a hot day. Oh, George, I guess there is some bad news. You drop your ice cream on the ground."

George smiled and gave a big sigh of relief.

"*That* was good news?" asked Janice.

"Yeah," said George. "It was daylight, and we were all okay. That means whatever happens tonight, we're going to live through it and buy ice cream sometime another day in the future."

Janice thought, *I wonder if Bridgette made that vision up. It doesn't sound real. Well, Bridgette, did you?*

"George, can you see if my mom is ready to drop us off?" asked Bridgette.

When George left the bedroom, Bridgette asked, "Janice, though it might even seem like a noble thing to do at this point in time, have you ever known me to lie to my friends?"

"No," replied Janice.

"Then don't even ask."

They heard Bridgette's mom rattling the keys and knew it was time to go. George entered back into the room and said, "Ready?"

"Yep," replied Bridgette, "Let's go walk like lions."

Chapter 39

Bridgette's mom dropped them off at the front entrance of the school. The street lights made it somewhat visible to see the outlines of the school and the darkened parking lot that led to the laboratory. The wind was gusting, making it feel colder than it actually was.

"It's a good thing your mom's staying out here in the parking lot in case we need a quick escape," said Janice.

"Uh, what exactly is the plan again?" asked George nervously.

"Mainly," said Bridgette, "it's to stop Ms. Leadbetter before she locks us up in one of those giant cubes like Janice's mom."

George looked at Janice. "Have you been practicing….. you know……with your new powers?"

"Still pretty weak," admitted Janice, "but I got these." She held up her hands and balled them up into fists. Then she nodded her head confidently.

"I don't know why," said George, "but I have more confidence in those fists than I do in my own abilities."

"You just lack courage, George," said Bridgette.

"If I had your abilities," said George, "I'd be roaring with courage."

Bridgette smiled. "Remember my vision, George. Somewhere in the future we will all be eating ice cream together. Whatever happens tonight can't be all that bad."

George straightened up and stuck his chest out a bit more and said, "You're right, and my powers have come a long way."

"That's the spirit," replied Bridgette. "Now let's go see if we can find Wanda and the Alpha."

They slinked over to the lab entrance door and looked around. The gigantic parking lot had four cars in it parked at different locations throughout. Two of the light posts were either broken or burned out, but for the most part, the parking lot was well lit. Near the building, however, the lights could not penetrate the darkness from such a distance. As a result, the kids had limited visibility near the buildings.

They walked up to the laboratory door and started speaking in low voices.

"Do you see anyone?" whispered George.

"Not yet," replied Janice, "but be quiet and listen. I thought I heard something coming from over there." She was pointing, but George couldn't see her hand, so he just listened.

From out of the darkness came a shiny light as bright as a flashlight, but everyone recognized it as a cell phone. It illuminated Wanda's face so the mystery of who was approaching was solved pretty quickly.

Wanda walked up to Bridgette and said, "You're late."

Bridgette checked her own cell phone. "It's 12:01."

"See," replied Wanda. She smiled and slugged Bridgette on the shoulder.

Bridgette looked at Janice. "Doesn't that seem like something you would do? I told you that you guys are more alike than you think."

Janice shrugged her shoulders, but the body language was lost in the dark.

"Thanks for coming, Wanda," said Bridgette.

"It's the least I could do," replied Wanda, "but I'm not sure how much help I will be if no one's asleep."

"Nonsense, we're a team and stronger together than apart," said Bridgette. "I know! Stay close to George and remind him to use his powers if and when we need them. Sometimes his fear clouds his mind." She glanced at George. "No offense, George."

"Offense taken," whined George. "What do you think I am? A coward?"

"Of course not," responded Bridgette. "I just meant that sometimes it's hard to think straight when you're in the heat of battle."

The word "battle" caused goosebumps to sprout all over his body. "Good idea. Stay close to me, Wanda. I'll protect you."

Almost everyone rolled their eyes, but, again, it was lost in the darkness.

The jingling of keys attracted everyone's attention. The sound was coming from inside the laboratory. A flashlight turned on, and the door clicked before opening.

"Janice, is that you, honey?"

Janice stepped in front of Bridgette to get to the door. "Hi, Dad. Are you alone?"

"Of course, honey. I said I would be." He waved his flashlight, motioning for everyone to enter. "I didn't turn on the lights because I don't want to attract any unwanted attention, especially from those security guards who think they're cops or something."

***

Officer Halfpenny spotted the light and the huddle of people near the lab. "You see that, Charlie?"

Charlie poked his head up so that he could see through the passenger's side window in the front seat of the car, a typical Toyota. They were in one of the cars that was resting in the school's parking lot.

"Keep your head down, you fool," complained Officer Halfpenny. "You tryin' to give us away?"

"Just doin' what you told me, Philip," replied Charlie. "How much are we getting from Leadbetter again?"

"I told you. Ain't gettin' nuttin' if Ms. Leadbetter spots us. We gots to show up at the right time.....just when she needs us."

"That doesn't make any sense," said Charlie.

"Don't have to," replied Philip. "Just follow my lead, and we be countin' Benjamins fo the night is over."

"I just want to count some money before this night is over."

"Man, shut up!" exclaimed Philip. "You a lot smarter when you quiet."

Charlie opened his mouth to say something but then closed his jaw and tightened it.

"Alright, they in the building now. Follow me all cat burglar-like." Philip cautiously opened his door, crawled out with his head hunched low, and then quietly clicked the door shut.

"Cat burglar-like," mumbled Charlie. "I ain't no dang cat. I'm a lion." He opened his door and silently departed the vehicle. "A lion who's going to get paid."

Philip looked toward the entrance where he saw Dr. Cooper let the others inside the building. He noticed a light shining on the door. "You see that, Charlie? Someone's-" He stopped talking as he had turned to look at Charlie who was shining his flashlight at the building. "What the heck, Charlie. You may as well be screaming to the world that you casin' the place."

Charlie shut his flashlight off. "Well, maybe if you told me more what we're doing here, I might be persuaded to act more like a cat-with-nine-lives burglar."

"Man, you don't make no sense."

They both hunched low and speed walked across the parking lot toward the building.

Once inside, they walked to their office and grabbed a large container. After making sure their remote controlled planes were inside, they both smiled and headed down the hallway, both sharing the weight of the box equally.

"Who's coming?" asked Charlie.

A loud clip clopping sound was walking toward them. They lowered the box to the floor so they could get a better look.

"What are you two doing here at *this* hour?" asked Ms. Leadbetter.

Officer Halfpenny said, "We could ask you the same thing, Ms.- "

"But you won't," said Ms. Leadbetter sharply, "because I ask the questions around here, not the hired help."

Not knowing too much about Ms. Leadbetter's abilities, Charlie started thinking, *This smart-mouthed lady needs to learn some manners.*

Ms. Leadbetter looked at Charlie. "And are you going to teach me some manners?"

Charlie looked at Philip dumbfounded.

"She can read minds, Charlie; I told you this befo."

Officer Halfpenny looked back at Ms. Leadbetter. "We was just gonna practice usin' these here remote controlled airplane taser weapons."

"Excellent idea," said Ms. Leadbetter. "In fact, I just might have someone you can *practice* on."

Officer Halfpenny tried to clarify. "Oh, I meant we was gonna practice usin' them so we could git better flyin' 'em. I didn't mean to say we was gonna practice usin' 'em on people."

"Silence," commanded Ms. Leadbetter. "What I have in mind, you'll be able to do both. She opened up her purse and pulled out two one hundred dollar bills. Handing one to Charlie and one to Philip, she said, take your drones or planes, whatever you want to call them, to the laboratory and wait in the back until you hear further instructions from me. *Do not* turn on the lights."

"Yes, ma'am," agreed Officer Halfpenny.

She walked away.

Officer Halfpenny said, "Charlie, look at yo money. What name is under that man's picture?"

Charlie unfolded the bill and read it. "Franklin."

"Das right, Charlie. *Benjamin* Franklin."

Charlie stood there for a moment, and then the light bulb finally went off. "Ohhhhh, I git it."

They picked up the box and continued heaving it to the lab.

Chapter 40

"Right this way," ladies and gentle*man*," said Dr. Cooper. He was wearing his white lab coat. "Let's go through my office so we can get to the main lab. There are plenty of chairs in there where we can chat."

The four students followed Janice's dad cautiously into the large laboratory. It smelled like animals and rat droppings.

"Gross!" exclaimed Wanda.

Bridgette put her fingers to her lips. "Shhhh."

Dr. Cooper opened the door from his office that led to the large warehouse sized laboratory. He turned on one light that lit up a small section of the area closest to them, right above a round meeting table. Without anyone noticing, he locked his office door before closing it behind them.

"Have a seat, everyone," said Dr. Cooper.

After everyone pulled out a chair and sat down, Dr. Cooper spoke first. "So, Janice, I suppose you are all wondering what's going on around here."

George looked out into the darkness across the huge open space. He could hear rats scratching and biting at their cages. He looked at Janice and waited for her response.

"Daddy, we're scared," replied Janice. "As you saw earlier today, Ms. Leadbetter is after us for something. What does she want?"

Dr. Cooper shifted slightly in his seat. "Honey, nobody's *after* anyone. This is all one big misunderstanding. She is only trying to make sure her data collection is accurate. Like if one of my lab rats escaped, I would want to find it to make sure I kept good notes. That's all that's going on here. She seems to think you guys are keeping your results private."

"Sorry to interrupt, Mr. Cooper," said Bridgette politely, "I think Janice is just asking what the purpose of these Mind over Matter experiments are for."

Dr. Cooper turned his head toward Bridgette. "Ahh, Bridgette, Ms. Leadbetter told me you were quite the inquisitive student, always asking questions about stuff you don't understand."

"Dad," whined Janice, "why can't you just tell us?"

Janet's dad continued to evade the question. "Let's say I discovered a cure for cancer, and you asked me how it worked. I could then go on about all the mechanisms in your immune system and t-cell counts, etcetera, etcetera. Because you are not scientists, and you are just kids, you would never understand the explanation. I realize Ms. Leadbetter has a certain way about her, and she may not be the most patient person in the world, but to explain rocket science to a student who doesn't even know what a rocket is...... well, that would be ludicrous."

"Try us," said Wanda. "We didn't get scholarships to this school for no reason."

"Why not ask her yourself?" suggested the doctor. He gazed across the room until Ms. Leadbetter's face swam through the darkness as she approached the table.

"I knew it!" shouted George. "We knew you couldn't be trusted." He scowled at Dr. Cooper.

"I'm sorry you feel that way, George," said Dr. Cooper. "A man would do anything for his daughter's safety."

"Daddy, what have you done?" cried Janice.

"He did what he was told," said Ms. Leadbetter arrogantly.

"What do you want?" demanded Bridgette.

"Still asking questions, huh, Bridgette? Come with me behind the red door, darling, and no one will get hurt," replied Ms. Leadbetter.

"That's not going to happen," said Bridgette. She stood from her chair and slowly raised her hands upward. Ms. Leadbetter's body lifted into the air and hovered about five feet off the floor. "Go get the police, guys. I'll hold her here."

Wanda rose from her chair and raced to Dr. Cooper's office door. She grabbed the doorknob and yanked. "It's locked!"

All eyes turned to Dr. Cooper.

199

"She's not trying to harm you, Bridgette," said Dr. Cooper.

While using one hand to keep Ms. Leadbetter suspended in air, Bridgette focused her other hand on the locked door. She pulled her arm toward her chest, and the door started trembling until it ripped from its hinges and fell to the floor.

Ms. Leadbetter's eyes lit up. "Very impressive, darling, but while you're just gaining your power, I've had mine for quite a while, and I know how to use it." She flew higher toward the ceiling and aimed her sights on Wanda.

Bridgette could feel her hold on her principal loosening.

Wanda's body began floating toward the ceiling. Once suspended, Ms. Leadbetter concentrated on Janice next. Janice kicked her legs frantically, yelling, "No! No!" She clenched her fists together. "Wait till I get my hands on you! You're gonna wish you were never born!"

"That's what I like about you, Janice," said Ms. Leadbetter. "You always speak your mind. No need to have to read it."

"Be careful with my daughter!" hollered Dr. Cooper.

She looked at George. "Georgie, you're next." His feet started lifting upward, but George closed his eyes and held his breath while trying to fight it.

"Leave my friends alone!" cried Bridgette.

"I got this, Bridge!" yelled George. His face turned as blue as a blueberry, but his feet stayed glued to the ground.

"You're doing it, George!" exclaimed Bridgette. "Keep it up!"

A few seconds later George let out a big gasp of air, and he instantly rose toward the ceiling. "Whoa!" He raised his hands to protect his head from crashing into the ceiling.

Bridgette raised her eyes and glared at Ms. Leadbetter who was under her own power now, levitating and controlling the three other students. As was usually the case, when Bridgett grew angry, a vision began to form inside her head.

This is inconvenient, she thought. She pushed the vision out of her head before it could really begin. She couldn't focus on the future when she needed to deal with the present. She raised her hands high and slowly started pulling them downward, almost like she had an invisible rope in her hand and was playing a game of tug-o-war. With each pull, Ms. Leadbetter came closer to the ground.

When Ms. Leadbetter knew she couldn't win, she screamed, "Release me at once, or I'll drop all of your friends! Surely, they'll break a leg or two at the very least."

George was trying to fight back mentally, but he was no match for Ms. Leadbetter, even when her powers were being divided as they were.

Bridgette hesitated like she didn't know what to do.

"Can't make up your mind?" said Ms. Leadbetter. "I'll do it for you. I'm going to drop the dream weaver girl first. Then maybe you'll see I mean business."

Wanda suddenly plummeted through the air, but Bridgette concentrated enough to slow her fall, landing her safely on the floor.

"How touching!" shouted Ms. Leadbetter. "But can you save two at a time?"

"Wait!" screamed Bridgette. She released her wicked principal back into the air again.

"That's more like it," said Ms. Leadbetter. "Now, we're going to try doing things *my* way."

Bridgette folded her arms. "And what is *your* way?"

Ms. Leadbetter dropped to the floor and walked into the darkness toward the center of the room. "Follow me, Bridgette."

"Uh, where are you going?" asked Bridgette

Behind the red door, thought Ms. Leadbetter.

"There's nothing up there but Janice's mom. Why would you need *me*?"

You're definitely needed, thought Ms. Leadbetter. *More than you know.*

"Can I save her somehow?" asked Bridgette with hope in her voice.

Come and find out, sweetie.

The floating kids descended safely to the floor. Once the last pair of shoes landed, Bridgette walked into the darkness toward the red door.

"Please help her," Dr. Cooper called out.

"Be careful, Bridgette," said Wanda. "It could be a trap."

"If you're not back in 10 minutes, we're coming after you," said George bravely.

"Maybe even sooner," said Janice.

"Don't worry, guys" said Bridgette. "Remember, we've got time on our side. The future's not etched in stone." She disappeared into the darkness.

"What did she mean by that?" asked Dr. Cooper."

"Uh, it's a private joke," responded George.

Chapter 41

"I'm worried," said George.

"It's only been five minutes so far, George," replied Wanda.

Dr. Cooper finally asked Wanda the question that had been bothering him the whole time. "I understand why the others are here, but why are you here?"

"Just helping out a friend," she responded. Then she looked at Janice and George and said, "Friends."

Janice looked at her father and said, "While we're alone, whose side are you on, *Dad*?"

Dr. Cooper sighed and said, "Ours, honey….yours, your mother's, *and* mine. I have to continue my research for your mother's sake, and now you're wrapped up into this experiment as well. I need Leadbetter's funding. Without it, we may never get your mother back. I can't lose hope….not now….not ever."

"Don't put your hope in money, Dad. Put your hope in Bridgette. *We* have."

George nodded his head. "She has a plan, and I trust her."

Wanda chimed in as well. "We were enemies just a couple of days ago, and now I'm here sticking my neck out for her. She has that effect on people."

"She saved my life, Dad," said Janice. "I thought I was a goner because I started getting headaches."

"So I was right to keep you locked up in the cellar," replied her dad.

Janice shook her head, and a tear escaped her eye. "No, Dad, that was still wrong. But it doesn't matter now. Bridgette knew what to do. I'm a better person now because of her."

"Eight minutes," said George.

"Let's go get her," said Janice. She stormed into the darkness, and they all followed.

When they exited the elevator on the basement floor, they could see Janice's mother inside her glass cube. She was sitting on the floor, twirling her hair with a finger while staring off into nothingness. Swiftly, but cautiously, they approached.

Upon arrival, they noticed a flashing of lights in the far corner of the room. It was Bridgette! She was sitting in a chair wearing a shiny silver helmet. Wires were connecting the helmet to some sort of power source, a metal box, located on the floor behind her. The helmet contained red, yellow, and green baby light bulbs that were blinking on and off with no particular pattern. Though it looked like she was staring straight ahead at them, she didn't blink her eyes or change her dull, lifeless, facial expression.

"Bridgette!" cried Janice. "What has she done to you?"

From behind Bridgette, a door to a small office opened up. "Ha! Ha! Ha! Ha! If you could have seen the looks on your faces when you saw little Miss Questionaire with her sci fi helmet on. Ha! Ha! Ha! Ha! Priceless, I tell you."

"Okay, Leadbetter," said Dr. Cooper, "I think you've taken this a bit too far."

"Surely, Dr. Cooper, you are jesting with me," replied Ms. Leadbetter. "Did you not do the same thing with your own daughter?"

"I didn't use that life-sucking helmet!" he spat back at her.

Ms. Leadbetter smiled. "Well, you should have. After all, you created it, and we know just how much you like to experiment on your own family.

"Now that I'm about to get what I want, I need to tie up any loose ends. She turned around and yelled, "Release the planes!"

From inside the small office, Officer Halfpenny replied, "Das what I'm talkin' 'bout." He punched a few buttons on his remote control module and said, "Charlie, git yer drone off the ground."

Two planes, each about a foot in length, buzzed into action.

"You need to stop this madness," said Dr. Cooper.

"I see you've chosen your side, *Janice's father*," said Ms. Leadbetter. "I should have known. No matter; you'll still work for me if you want to continue your research."

The small planes buzzed around the room like a couple of wild bees whose nest was just destroyed.

Wanda hid behind George. "Okay, Whiz, let's see some of that cool stuff you've been learning. Show us your courage and power."

Just as soon as the words left her mouth, one plane locked onto George, but he bravely faced the plane while concentrating on throwing it off course. He swung his head to the side, and the plane zoomed toward the wall and exploded upon impact.

"Ha! Ha! You're gonna have to do better than these little toys," bragged George.

Right after the words left his mouth, another plane ambushed him from the side. It wasn't that close, and it didn't need to be. It fired a few strong bolts of electricity at George, which zapped him in the shirt. They sparked and smoked while George's body locked up and fell to the ground. He lay on the floor screaming, "I can't move!"

Ms. Leadbetter ran up to George. "Quick! "We need another helmet for this one!"

Officer Halfpenny dropped his remote control and started rummaging through some boxes that were hidden in the closet. After searching the second box, he yelled, "Eureka! Got one!" He ran out of the office with a similar helmet containing long dangling wires. "You want I should take off these blinking lights?"

"No, you idiot! Just bring it over here!" She was standing over George.

Officer Halfpenny said with an angry voice, "Now wait just a minute. You may have introducted me to Ben Franklin this evening, but dat don't give you no right to disrespect me in front of my peers. Ain't dat right, Charlie?"

Charlie was standing only a few feet away. "That's right, Philip. No woman's going to disrespect us for just a hundred dollars."

"How about three hundred," replied Ms. Leadbetter.

Charlie smiled. "Now for that, you can even talk about my momma."

"May I have the helmet now, please!" cried Ms. Leadbetter.

Charlie ran across the room and tried to hand the helmet full of blinking lights to her.

"It's not for me, you fool!" barked Ms Leadbetter. "Place it on his head."

Charlie looked up and said, "Hey, Philip, give me a hand over here."

Ms. Leadbetter frowned. "Are you kidding me? Do you not know how to put a helmet on someone's head? What am I paying you for? Give me that! I'll do it myself." She snatched the helmet from his hand, wires dragging on the ground.

George looked up at her, lying on the floor like a turtle turned over on its shell, not able to move or even wiggle his body. "Get that thing away from me!"

Ms. Leadbetter leaned down and said, "Don't worry, darling. I have a consent form signed by your parents for this. Ha! Ha! Ha! Ha!"

"No!!!"

She placed the helmet on his head and said to Charlie, "Can you at least carry the boy over to the chair next to the girl?"

Charlie reached down to pick up George, but before he could stand with him in his arms, Wanda leaped onto his back.

"You're not taking him anywhere!" yelled Wanda.

Ms. Leadbetter smiled and said, "I admire your spunk, little Miss *Nightmare*, but you need to stop interfering with my plans." She lifted one hand in the air, and instantly Wanda started floating upward.

Wanda grasped her hands together around Charlie's neck to help anchor herself to the floor. It helped for a few seconds, but her fingers were beginning to slip apart. "No!" she cried. "I can't hold on much longer, George! You don't need to be able to move to use your mind. Fight back!"

Instead of focusing on trying to hold Wanda to the ground, George decided this time to go straight to the source of trouble. He gazed up at Ms. Leadbetter and noticed a large fan hovering above her head. Angrily he glared at the fan, trying to force it to drop from the ceiling. By not attacking Ms. Leadbetter directly, he was able to surprise her.

"George!" yelped Wanda. Her fingers came apart, and she started floating upward.

In the same instant the fan let go of the ceiling and came crashing down on Ms. Leadbetter. Just before it hit her, she noticed it and was able to cradle her head with her arms before the impact. She collapsed to the ground with the big fan lying on top of her.

Her hold on Wanda was released, causing Wanda to fall three feet to the floor. Like a spry cat, she landed on her feet.

"Get this thing off of me!" yelled Ms. Leadbetter.

Charlie let go of George to rescue Ms Leadbetter from the fan, which gave Wanda her chance to drag George into the office to hide.

Janice had been waiting for an opportunity to make a break for Bridgette, and the falling fan was it. She dodged the plane and raced to her friend. Standing in front of her she said, "Bridgette, can you hear me?"

Bridgette didn't respond. She stared blankly ahead as if she were in a coma with her eyes open.

Instinctively, Janice grabbed the helmet and was about to jerk if off her head, but fearful it may harm her friend, she decided against it. She noticed the cords coming out of the helmet were plugged into a metal box so she reached down and unplugged them. The moment the cords came out of the box, Bridgette blinked her eyes and slowly started moving again.

"Bridgette!" exclaimed Janice. "You're awake!"

"Thanks, Janice," responded Bridgette. "Now let's go finish this."

The plane that was chasing Janice now locked on to its next target: Bridgette. It flew straight at her and then fired two shots of electricity. Bridgette stared at the two bolts, persuading them to turn around and target Officer Halfpenny, the one in control of the plane. He dropped his remote control box and started running across the floor, but he wasn't fast enough. When they zapped him in the back, his muscles locked up, and he fell to the floor in convulsions.

"One down, two to go," cheered Bridgette.

Charlie finally removed the heavy fan from Ms. Leadbetter's body. "Well, at least you have *one* fan."

Ms. Leadbetter snarled. "Your attempt at humor is not appreciated." She waved her hand, and Charlie stumbled to the side. "Out of my way, fool."

Just then Dr. Cooper entered the scene. He witnessed the look on Ms. Leadbetter's face and feared for his daughter's life. "Don't worry, honey. Daddy's here."

Meanwhile the drone had swooped around and was heading for Bridgette and Janice. It fired two more shots. The bolts zigzagged through the air, searching for their mark, and now that Dr. Cooper was in the vicinity, Ms. Leadbetter took control of the dangerous electricity with her eyes and led the charges right to Dr. Cooper.

"Daddy, look out!" screamed Janice.

Dr. Cooper turned around just in time for the electricity to zap him directly in the chest.

The blood rushed out of Janice's face leaving it ghostly white. "Daddy!"

Dr. Cooper fell to the ground in a fit of convulsions.

Janice raced to his side.

Bridgette would have come too, but she had Ms. Leadbetter in her sights.

Janice fell to her knees and spilled her tears on her father's lab coat. "Daddy, your pacemaker. Are you alright?"

Her dad was breathing heavily with much labor. "I love you, Janice. Look after your mother. Don't give up hope."

"I, I don't understand," said Janice. "Why are you saying this? You're gonna be alright."

Dr. Cooper took a few quick puffs of air and said, "There isn't much time. Listen to me. You need to know something, but you can't tell Bridgette." He closed his eyes and winced in pain.

Janice, while weeping, leaned over and placed an ear over her dad's mouth. "What is it?"

He lifted his head so his daughter could hear. His voice was weakening. "Bridgette was only given a placebo."

"A what?" asked Janice.

"She and a couple of other students did not receive the serum like you and George."

Janice shook her head. "That's not true. I saw her get the shot, just like everyone else."

Her dad let out a long breath. "That was a harmless saline solution."

Janice was stunned. "You mean......she's doing all this stuff by herself?"

"She's a special child," he answered. He let out a final breath, and then the light in his eyes faded.

"Daddy, no, I can't lose you too," she cried. "I can't. What will happen to me now? I need you. Come back to me. What about Mom? You have to save Mom." Teary eyed, she looked up at the transparent cube where her mom was imprisoned.

Chapter 42

Charlie and Ms. Leadbetter were standing side by side. They saw Philip barely moving on the ground, obviously in no shape to continue the fight, and they watched Janice walk slowly in a daze toward the transparent cube where her mom was caged.

Ms. Leadbetter said to Charlie, "Go after the other two. Bridgette is all mine."

Charlie threw down the remote control and removed his taser from his holster. "I'm going to enjoy this."

"Now!" yelled Wanda. With George leaning against her, they hobbled together toward the elevator.

Charlie caught the movement from the corner of his eye and raced toward them, taser in hand.

The elevator door closed just as he reached them.

He looked around and said, "This is a dangerous setup. No stairs." He pushed the button and waited for the elevator to come back.

Seconds later the bell rang, and doors opened up again. He jumped inside and pushed the button to go up.

George and Wanda heard the bell ring again, which means they knew Charlie followed them back up to the first level. They stayed hidden on the dark side of the warehouse, the side away from the lit up room where they had sat earlier at the round table.

Charlie cautiously searched the area, the way he had been trained before he became a security guard, which was only a one-day training session. He held a flashlight in one hand and his taser in the other. Stepping as if he might step on a land mine at any moment he continued his search.

George and Wanda were hunched low behind a long table of rat cages. Charlie was walking away from them until one of the rats started gnawing on its cage. Charlie heard it and turned his head.

"Sounds like I heard me a couple of rats," he called out. "Have no fear; the rat patrol is on the case."

Wanda and George had to stay where they were because they wouldn't be able to outrun Charlie, not with George's extremities barely functioning. The recovery time for a blast from a powerful droid was much longer than from a hand held taser.

Charlie stepped closer, listening for the slightest sound of movement. Sure enough, the rat started biting its cage again, leading him even closer to it and to Wanda and George.

"Come out, come out, wherever you are!"

Wanda and George both squeezed their eyes shut, hoping they wouldn't be seen. They could hear his breathing, probably because he was a smoker. He must have been only a few feet away.

"Well, look what the cat dragged in," said Charlie.

They opened their eyes. Charlie was smiling and pointing his taser at them.

Wanda glared at him. "You better not shoot us if you know what's good for you."

"Oh, I know what's good for me," said Charlie. "It's called money. How much you got?"

"As if!" exclaimed Wanda.

George gulped. "Uh, I have an emergency credit card that my parents gave me."

Charlie shook his head. "What do I look like? A cash machine?"

"Do something, Whiz," said Wanda.

George stared at Charlie intensely until he started lifting off the ground.

Charlie panicked and shot his taser at George. Upon impact George fell to the ground and started shaking.

Wanda kneeled down to comfort him.

Charlie landed on his feet and said, "I'd have shot you sooner if I knew you could do that. I thought only the girl upstairs had that kind of power." He looked back at Wanda. "You must have the power too." He raised his gun and pointed it at her.

Before he could pull the trigger, however, two hands lunged from out of the darkness and grabbed a hold of Charlie's neck.

Charlie looked down at the large hands. "What the heck!"

"The Alpha!" shouted Wanda, loud enough to let George know what was going on.

Charlie, gasping for breath, dropped his taser.

Wanda crawled over and grabbed it. "Sorry, Charlie." She pointed it at him and watched him try to claw backwards at the Alpha with no success. He kicked and struggled until finally his body went limp. The Alpha released him, allowing him to collapse to the ground. Hesitantly, Wanda crept toward the body and stared at Charlie's stomach.

"Is he.....?" asked George.

"No, he's still breathing," replied Wanda. She turned and looked up at the Alpha. "Thank you."

The Alpha nodded his head and backed into the blanket of darkness, vanishing before their very eyes.

"How do you feel, George?" asked Wanda.

"That taser felt more like a shock compared to the droid upstairs. Still, I'm weak, though I hate to admit it."

"Well, I don't think we'll do Bridgette any good upstairs if we go back up there. Ms. Leadbetter will just use us again to get to her."

"I hope she and Janice are okay," said George.

***

Janice seemed to be in a trance. After her father dying right in front of her, she felt like she had lost everything. Her mom was her last drop of hope. In a zombie-like walk she made her way to her mother's cell. She reached for the doorknob. Locked. Angrily, she pounded at the door.

The noise grabbed her mother's attention. She wandered to the door and put her ear to it and listened.

Meanwhile, Ms. Leadbetter and Bridgette were having a battle of the minds. They were flying around the room, willing each other to slam against the walls of the building. They were like magnets repelling against each other.

Learning from what George had done to her earlier, Ms. Leadbetter tried a bit of trickery. She concentrated on a wooden chair and hurled it at Bridgette, who was caught off guard. The chair struck her in the back and splintered into several pieces. Bridgette lost her focus and fell from the air and crashed hard to the floor. Having the wind knocked out of her, she sat on her hands and knees, trying desperately to catch her breath, while tears streamed down her cheeks.

"Face it, Bridgette! You're no match for me!" bragged Ms. Leadbetter.

Bridgette stood slowly and tightened her fists. She was furious, and a vision ensued. She only needed to see a glimpse of it before she knew what to do. She unleashed all of her anger with one thrust of her arms in Ms. Leadbetter's direction. An overwhelming force, like a strong gust of wind but with the power of a hurricane, flew out of Bridgette's hands, upward toward the flying Ms. Leadbetter. The supersonic wave of energy tossed her wicked principal against the wall so hard it made a dent in the shape of her body. She stuck for a moment before falling to the ground where she lay unconscious.

Bridgette rolled over and lay on her back, wincing from pain. She placed a hand on her side and said, "Ow!" Slowly, she sat up to listen more carefully. She could hear someone's thoughts.

I'm coming, Mom.

"Janice!" screamed Bridgette. She rose to her feet and trudged toward the large cell. "Janice! Don't go in there! It's too dangerous!"

Janice was slamming a chair against the glass wall. The chair broke into pieces, so she snatched up a wooden leg and began beating the doorknob with it. She bashed and bashed until the knob fell to the floor. The door cracked open and Janice entered.

"Janice! No!" cried Bridgette.

Janice met her mother in the doorway. Her mom stood there showing no emotion, not even curiosity about this person, her own daughter, standing in front of her.

Not knowing what to do, Bridgette stood outside the room and watched.

Janice stepped up to her mother and said, "Mommy?"
Nothing.

"Mommy, please," cried Janice. She reached out for her mother.

"Agggg!" grunted her mom. She shrugged away from Janice's approach.

Tears flowed down Janice's cheeks. "Mommy, you're all I've got. Daddy…..Daddy's dead." She reached out and hugged her, this time clinging onto her mother's back.

Her mother twisted and turned trying to escape the embrace.

Bridgette's eyes grew glossy until the tears came.

If only there were something I could do, she thought.

Suddenly, she was reminded by her own thoughts of the recent past. A vision of her speaking to Wanda formed in her head. Wanda was shaking her head saying, "Dang, is there anything you can't do?"

And another vision of Wanda played out as well. "You think that's possible?" Wanda had asked. And she, Bridgette, had replied by saying, "All things are possible."

After gaining the confidence she needed, Bridgette, through teary-eyed, blurry vision, concentrated on Janice's mom. She held out her hands and focused. Her body started to tremble. She blinked and the tears rolled down her cheeks, but she held her concentration. She could barely see because her tears clouded her line of sight. She didn't give up though. She couldn't. She knew somewhere deep within her being that she could do this.

It was a subtle change at first. Janice's mother stopped struggling to break from Janice's grasp. She stood there, allowing herself to be hugged.

And then all at once an explosion of feeling came over Janice. Her mom had begun to hug her back.

Janice pulled away for a second to look at her. "Mommy? Is that you?"

Her mother's face was back to normal. "I've missed you so much, sweetie," said her mom. She was bawling so much, her body was shaking.

214

Janice smiled and hugged her mother tightly. "I missed you too."

While hugging, they managed to turn their bodies toward the doorway where they witnessed Bridgette with her arms stretched toward them before she finally passed out on the floor.

Chapter 43

Thirty minutes later Bridgette woke up. She was resting downstairs on the round table.

"She's awake!" screamed George.

They all walked over to greet her.

"What's going on?" asked Bridgette.

"Your mom called the police," said Wanda. "The *real* police. She's outside right now watching them haul away those security guards *and* Ms. Leadbetter."

"I've got to see this," said Bridgette.

She slid off the table and walked through the office door to the outside.

Two police cars and an ambulance were parked out front with their lights twirling. Another ambulance had already taken off carrying Janice's mom to the hospital. Philip and Charlie were being handcuffed and placed in the back of one of the cars. Ms. Leadbetter was still unconscious, so she was lying on a stretcher. Two men were carrying her toward the back of the ambulance.

While the paramedics were getting ready to place Ms. Leadbetter inside, the loud sound of a helicopter could be heard roaring in the distance, approaching at an alarming rate. Everyone, including the police, were looking upward into the dark night. The dark aircraft with blinking red lights descended upon them about twenty feet in the air. Although Ms. Leadbetter was unconscious, somehow she and the stretcher she was lying on began to float upward toward the helicopter.

Bridgette's mouth gaped open. "This can't be happening. It isn't fair."

Instantly, she began receiving a vision of the future. Ms. Leadbetter was inside the helicopter, and she was just figuring out who her rescuers were.

"Mom and Dad! But how did you know…..?" began Ms. Leadbetter.

216

"We've been watching you," replied her mother.

"And we like what we've seen," said her father.

Ms. Leadbetter's eyes glossed over. "That's all I've ever wanted. It's all I've been working for..... a chance to show you that I'm important....that I matter.....and that I'm not a nuisance."

"We're sorry we neglected you those many years ago," said her father. "We were so caught up in our work. It's complete now, and we want you to share in our success."

"Who do you think it was?" asked George after the helicopter had flown off.

Bridgette shook her head, waking from her vision. "It was her parents," she replied.

"Oh, you were just having a vision, weren't you? Sorry, I thought you just looked tired from everything that went down tonight."

"That's okay, Whiz. I saw what I needed to know."

Bridgette's mom walked up to the group. "Come on, kids. Let's go home."

***

Pending an investigation, the school was shut down for the duration of the week, which gave Bridgette the time she needed to rescue all the Berserkers. For the next few days Bridgette spent all of her time curing the Alpha, Sissy, and the rest of the Berserkers living in the barrel towns.

The following week while George, Janice, and Bridgette were walking down the hallway after leaving their last class, Bridgette said, "It sure was nice of the school to let us keep our scholarships, even though they shut down the program."

"Sure was," replied George. He was suspending a red apple above the palm of his hand, his way of practicing his powers.

"Hey, I've got an idea!" shouted Janice. "Let's go get some ice cream."

"Who can say no to ice cream?" said Bridgette. "Come on, I'm buying."

They walked across the street to the ice cream parlor.

After ordering their favorite cones, they walked outside and started heading back toward the school.

"It sure is a hot day," said Janice.

Bridgette licked her cone and said, "So delicious, don't you think so, George?"

George went to lick his cone as well, but Bridgette quickly swatted the cone out of his hand, and it splattered on the ground.

George's mouth opened wide. "What did you do *that* for?"

Bridgette smirked. "Sorry, George, you can't fight the future." She looked up at the sky with a happy smile.

Other books by Eric Patterson

Something Lurking in the Bell Tower
The Legend of Skylar Swift, the Fastest Boy on Earth
Carl *Nose* the Truth
Fluffy, a Puppy with a Purpose
Nature Boy
Nature Boy: Nature Strikes Back